CONTENTS

CONTENTS

For Daniel Searle

INTRODUCTION

Most of the books that I'll be telling you about have one particular character in them who is either funny, interesting, or simply so *nice* that you'll want to know more about them and will look out for the books that tell *all* their stories. That is why I've called this one *Meet My Friends*, because I hope that – after you've read about them – they'll become *your* friends too.

I hope they will keep popping into your mind when certain things happen; for instance, when you see a little woman walking along on a windy day, you might think: 'She's like Mrs Pepperpot. Wouldn't it be awful if she grew even smaller and was blown away?' Or you might notice a black kitten with a white paw and you'll think of Gobbolino (that kitten may have blue eyes too!), and I'm pretty sure that even grown-ups will feel differently about guinea-pigs if you let them read *Olga Takes Charge*.

The pieces here are not all from new books: some of them, like *Milly-Molly-Mandy*, have been in print for such a long time that your grandmother may have read them when *she* was young. But because they have been so loved, they've gone on being reprinted, and may, like *The Wind in the Willows*, last for ever and ever, or at least long enough for you to read them to *your* children. So although you won't enjoy all of them exactly the same amount, I hope you'll find at least ten friends who will stay with you for the rest of your life.

K.W.

THE LAST SLICE OF RAINBOW

JOAN AIKEN

Illustrated by Margaret Walty

There are nine stories in this book: about Jason, who finds a rainbow; Clem, who loses a dream; Tim, who is shrunk by a goblin; Christina, a princess with magical hair; Polly, who is so sweet that even the Oak Tree loves her; Cal, who loses his legs; Michael, who paints wonderful pictures; Hattie, who saves all the spiders in the bath; and Dan, who invents magic words. You'll have a lovely time reading them. Here's Jason's story to start you off:

●

Jason walked home from school every day along the side of a steep grassy valley, where harebells grew and sheep nibbled. As he walked, he always whistled. Jason could whistle more tunes than anybody else at school, and he could remember every tune that he had ever heard. That was because he had been born in a windmill, just at the moment when the wind changed from south to west. He could see the wind as it blew; and that is a thing not many people can do. He could see patterns in the stars, too, and hear the sea muttering charms as it crept up the beach.

One day, as Jason walked home along the grassy path, he heard the west wind wailing and sighing. 'Oh, woe, woe! Oh, bother and blow! I've forgotten how it goes!'

'What have you forgotten, Wind?' asked Jason, turning to look at the wind. It was all brown and blue and wavery, with splashes of gold.

'My tune! I've forgotten my favourite tune! Oh, woe and blow!'

'The one that goes like this?' said Jason, and he whistled.

The wind was delighted. 'That's it! That's the one! Clever Jason!' And it flipped about him, teasing but kindly, turning up his collar, ruffling his hair. 'I'll give you a present,' it sang, to the tune Jason had whistled. 'What shall it be? A golden lock and a silver key?'

Jason couldn't think what use in the world *those* things would be, so he said quickly, 'Oh, please, I'd like a rainbow of my very own to keep.'

For, in the grassy valley, there were often beautiful rainbows to be seen, but they never lasted long enough for Jason.

'A rainbow of your own? That's a hard one,' said the wind. 'A very hard one. You must take a pail and walk up over the moor until you come to Peacock Force. Catch a whole pailful of spray from the waterfall. That will take you a long time. But when you have the pail full to the brim, you may find somebody in it who might be willing to give you a rainbow.'

Luckily the next day was Saturday. Jason took a

pail, and his lunch, and walked over the moor till he came to the waterfall that was called Peacock Force, because the water, as it dashed over the cliff, made a cloud of spray in which wonderful peacock colours shone and glimmered.

All day Jason stood by the fall, getting soaked, catching the spray in his pail. At last, just at sunset, he had the whole pail filled, right to the brim. And now, in the pail, he saw something that swam swiftly round and round — something that glimmered in brilliant rainbow colours.

It was a small fish.

'Who are you?' said Jason.

'I am the Genius of the Waterfall. Put me back! You have no right to keep me. Put me back and I'll reward you with a gift.'

'Yes,' said Jason quickly, 'yes, I'll put you back, and please may I have a rainbow of my very own, to keep in my pocket.'

'Humph!' said the Genius. 'I'll give you a rainbow, but whether you will be able to keep it is another matter. Rainbows are not easy to keep. I'll be surprised if you can even carry it home. However, here you are.'

And the Genius leapt out of Jason's pail, in a high soaring leap, back into its waterfall, and, as it did so, a rainbow poured out of the spray and into Jason's pail, following the course of the fish's leap.

'Oh, how beautiful!' breathed Jason, and he took

the rainbow from the pail, holding it in his two hands like a scarf, and gazed at its dazzling colours. Then he rolled it up carefully and put it in his pocket.

He started walking home.

There was a wood on his way, and in a dark place among the trees he heard somebody crying pitifully. He went to see what was the matter, and found a badger in a trap.

'Boy, dear, dear boy,' groaned the badger, 'let me out, let me out, or men will come with dogs and kill me.'

'How can I let you out? I'd be glad to, but the trap needs a key.'

'Push in the end of that rainbow I can see in your pocket, and you'll be able to wedge open the trap.'

Sure enough, when Jason pushed the end of the rainbow between the jaws of the trap, they sprang open, and the badger was able to clamber out. He made off at a lumbering trot, before the men and dogs could come. 'Thanks, thanks,' he gasped over his shoulder – then he was gone, down his hole.

Jason rolled up the rainbow and put it back in his pocket; but a large piece had been torn off by the sharp teeth of the trap and it blew away.

On the edge of the wood was a little house where old Mrs Widdows lived. She had a very sour nature. If children's balls bounced into her garden, she baked them in her oven until they turned to coal. Everything she ate was black – burnt toast, black tea, black

pudding, black olives. She called to Jason, 'Boy, will you give me a piece of that rainbow I see sticking out of your pocket? I'm very ill. The doctor says I need a rainbow pudding to make me better.'

Jason didn't much want to give Mrs Widdows a piece of his rainbow; but she did look ill and poorly, so, rather slowly, he walked into her kitchen, where she cut off a large bit of the rainbow with a breadknife. Then she made a stiff batter, with hot milk and flour and a pinch of salt, stirred in the piece of rainbow, and cooked the mixture. She let it get cold and cut it into slices and ate them with butter and sugar. Jason had a small slice too. It was delicious.

'That's the best thing I've eaten for a year,' said Mrs Widdows. 'I'm tired of black bread and black coffee and black grapes. I can feel this pudding doing me good.'

She did look better. Her cheeks were pink and she almost smiled. As for Jason, after he had eaten his small slice of pudding, he grew eight centimetres.

'You'd better not have any more,' said Mrs Widdows.

Jason put the last piece of rainbow back in his pocket.

There wasn't a lot left now.

As he drew near the windmill where he lived, his sister Tilly ran out to meet him. She tripped over a rock and fell, gashing her leg. Blood poured out of it, and Tilly, who was only four, began to wail. 'Oh, oh, my leg, my leg, my leg! It hurts dreadfully. Oh Jason, please bandage it, *please!*'

Well, what could he do? Jason pulled the rest of the rainbow from his pocket and wrapped it round Tilly's leg. There was just enough. He tore off a tiny scrap which he kept in his hand.

Tilly was in rapture with the rainbow round her leg. 'Oh! How beautiful! And it has quite stopped the bleeding!' She danced away to show everybody her wonderful rainbow-coloured leg.

Jason was left looking rather sadly at the tiny shred of rainbow between his thumb and finger. He heard a whisper in his ear, and turned to see the west wind frolicking about the hillside, all yellow and brown and rose-coloured.

'Well?' said the west wind. 'The Genius of the Waterfall did warn you that rainbows are hard to keep! And, even without a rainbow, you are a very lucky boy. You can see the pattern of the stars, and hear my song, and you have grown eight centimetres in one day.'

'That's true,' said Jason.

'Hold out your hand,' said the wind.

Jason held out his hand, with the piece of rainbow in it, and the wind blew, as you blow

17

on a fire to make it burn bright. As it blew, the piece of rainbow grew and grew, from Jason's palm, until it lifted up, arching into the topmost corner of the sky; not just a single rainbow, but a double one, with a second rainbow underneath *that*, the biggest and most brilliant that Jason had ever beheld. Many birds were so astonished at the sight that they stopped flying and fell to the ground, or collided with each other in mid-air.

Then the rainbow melted and was gone.

'Never mind!' said the west wind. 'There will be another rainbow tomorrow; or if not tomorrow, next week.'

'And I *did* have it in my pocket,' said Jason.

Then he went in for his tea.

●

Joan Aiken has written four other books of short stories you'll enjoy. They are called *The Kingdom Under the Sea*, *A Necklace of Raindrops*, *Past Eight O'Clock* and *Tale of a One-Way Street*.

THE LITTLE GIRL AND THE TINY DOLL

AINGELDA ARDIZZONE

Illustrated by Edward Ardizzone

The heroine of this story is The Little Girl, because she was so kind to The Tiny Doll. This is how it happened! A not-at-all nice little girl dropped The Tiny Doll into a deep freeze box all among the vegetables and fruit but no one noticed, and she was so tiny that she couldn't get out.

So she had to live there, eating the frozen strawberries and playing catch with the frozen peas. Poor Tiny Doll — she was very bored and lonely and very, very cold — that is, until The Little Girl saw her. After that life became quite exciting for both of them. Here's a little bit of what happened:

●

The doll looked so cold and lonely, but the girl did not dare to pick her up because she had been told not to touch things in the shop.

However, she felt she must do something to help the doll and as soon as she got home she set to work to make her some warm clothes.

First of all, she made her a warm bonnet out of a piece of red flannel. This was a nice and easy thing to start with.

After tea that day she asked mother to help her cut
out a coat from a piece of blue velvet.

She stitched away so hard that she had just time to
finish it before she went to bed.

It was very beautiful.

The next day her mother said they were going shopping, so the little girl put the coat and bonnet in an
empty matchbox and tied it into a neat parcel with
brown paper and string.

She held the parcel tightly in her hand as she

walked along the street, hurrying as she went. She longed to know if the tiny doll would still be there.

As soon as she reached the shop she ran straight to the deep freeze to look for her.

At first she could not see her anywhere. Then, suddenly, she saw her, right at the back, playing with the peas.

The tiny doll was throwing them into the air and hitting them with an ice-cream spoon.

It was a very dull game but it was something to do.

The little girl threw in the parcel and the doll at once started to untie it.

She looked very pleased when she saw what was inside.

She tried on the coat, and it fitted. She tried on the bonnet and it fitted too. She was very pleased.

She jumped up and down with excitement and waved to the little girl to say thank you.

She felt so much better in warm clothes and it made her feel happy to think that somebody cared for her.

Then she had an idea. She made the matchbox into a bed and pretended that the brown paper was a great big blanket.

With the string she wove a mat to go beside the bed.

At last she settled down in the matchbox, wrapped herself in the brown paper blanket and went to sleep.

THE RAILWAY CAT AND THE HORSE

PHYLLIS ARKLE

Illustrated by Lynne Byrnes

Alfie started out by being a humble, grateful sort of cat; pleased to hang about the station and encourage his friend Fred, the porter, even though Hack, the railman, thought he was a spoilt nuisance and tried to get him kidnapped. But he became more independent and brave after he had done a few noble deeds, like saving a passenger from a runaway train *and* becoming a TV personality.

In this story, taken from *The Railway Cat and the Horse*, he is saving a valuable antique from being stolen.

●

Mr Brock rose early next morning. Alfie stretched out and clenched and unclenched his claws before rolling over and falling off the camp-bed.

Mr Brock laughed. 'Come on, sleepy-head,' he said, 'this is an important day. First breakfast, then I'll finish work on Rex.'

'Miaow!' cried Alfie. Feeling very excited he joined the rocking-horse mender for breakfast in the house. Back in the workshop after the meal, Mr Brock walked round the old horse and studied him from every angle. 'There's only one more job to be done,' he announced. 'What's that, Alfie?'

'Miaow!' sang Alfie. He's minus mane and tail, of course.

'A new mane and tail for Rex,' said Mr Brock, smiling.

He picked up some long black horsehair, and made a mane for the horse, shaping it to fit down the neck. Then he cut some more horsehair for a tail. When these had been securely fixed and the rocking-horse mender could find nothing more to be done, he phoned the station and asked Fred to come along to the workshop.

Fred soon arrived, with Hack. 'I wasn't going to miss this,' said Hack.

'My word, Mr Brock, you have done a marvellous job,' said Fred as he stood back to admire the rocking-horse. He turned to Hack. 'Fit for a junk shop, did you say, Hack? Are you now prepared to eat your words?'

Hack grinned. 'All right, I'll have words for my supper tonight,' he said.

'I've enjoyed every minute of working on Rex,' said Mr Brock, 'and the thought of him leaving the country makes me shudder. I wouldn't mind so much if he was going back to his old home.'

'It's a shame he's got to be sold,' said Fred. 'But, whatever happens to him, I hope he will continue to give pleasure to children – and to grown-ups.'

'We'll all miss you, Rex,' said Hack as he gave the horse a friendly pat.

Fred looked at his watch. 'Time to go back to work,' he said. 'Day after tomorrow, Mr Brock, we'll collect Rex for his train journey to the auction rooms. In the meantime, it would be a good idea if you lined the bottom of the crate with more shavings.'

'I'll see to that,' promised Mr Brock as he opened the door for them. 'Staying, Alfie?'

'Miaow!' said Alfie. Please.

After breakfast next morning they returned to the workshop. Mr Brock examined the empty crate still standing in a corner. 'It does need more packing,' he said. He let down the side opening of the crate and started to bundle in shavings, sawdust and rolled-up papers. 'It wouldn't do to risk Rex being damaged in transit and spoiling all my hard work,' he said.

Alfie jumped into the crate and vigorously kneaded the packing with his paws. Then he curled up in the hollow he had made and looked up at Mr Brock.

'Miaow!' he said. It's very comfortable in here.

'Come out of there, Alfie,' laughed Mr Brock. 'We don't want to lose you as well as Rex.' Alfie pushed his nose right down between his paws. 'Now then, you heard me. Out you come,' coaxed Mr Brock.

Alfie was just about to oblige when there was a sharp rap on the door and two men, both in overalls, entered the workshop. Alfie stayed where he was.

'Good morning, Mr Brock,' said one man.

Alfie peeped out of the crate and immediately recognized the men who had asked Hack so many questions, and whom Alfie had observed walking slowly past Mr Brock's. This could be catastrophic, thought the railway cat!

'There's been a change of plan,' the man continued. 'The old rocking-horse is wanted at the auction rooms a day earlier, so instead of going by rail tomorrow we have been ordered to transport him by road *today*.'

Mr Brock looked bewildered as the man handed him a document. 'Here you are,' he said. 'Authority to collect one antique rocking-horse, name of Rex.'

The rocking-horse mender glanced at the paper. 'This seems to be in order,' he said slowly, 'but Fred didn't say anything about it yesterday.'

'He didn't know about it then,' was the reply. 'Reason for the change of plan is that there will be a wealthy bidder at tomorrow's auction, and the horse must be there in good time.'

'I'd prefer to get in touch with Fred, if you don't mind,' said Mr Brock, in a flurry.

'No need for that,' said the man sharply. 'Please give us a hand with the crate. We've brought a truck along with us.'

Alfie, almost hidden by the packing, crouched in a corner of the crate as the loading took place. He only just managed to escape being flattened by the rockers. He shook with fright as the crate, with himself and Rex inside, was securely fastened, then wheeled down the passage and lifted into a waiting van.

One man jumped into the driving seat, the other

into the passenger seat and within half a minute they were off. Not for one moment did Alfie believe they were bound for the auction rooms. He had thought these men looked untrustworthy when he had first set eyes on them at the station, and he had been proved right. What would happen to Rex – and to Alfie himself?

Mr Brock had been duped. Somehow the robbers had managed to obtain all the information required for them to steal Rex at the right moment. With his ear towards a crack in the side of the crate, Alfie caught snatches of the men's conversation.

'That was a piece of cake!' laughed the driver.

'You're telling me,' said the other. 'We'll be at the airport in record time. Soon this old rocking-horse will be thousands of miles away, and we'll collect a generous rake-off.'

Alfie felt trapped and helpless. The van was driven at speed but occasionally had to slow down. When he could, to relieve his tension, Alfie reached up and clawed at a very small splinter of wood which he had noticed underneath Rex's belly. After what seemed ages the van suddenly pulled up with a jerk and Alfie fell down flat.

'Keep calm, it's the police!' he heard the driver hiss to his mate.

The rear van door was thrown open and someone – must be a policeman, thought Alfie – climbed in and called out, 'We're checking all vehicles.' Alfie jumped as he heard a sharp rap on the side of the crate. 'What have you got inside here?' said the policeman.

'A refrigerator,' was the driver's prompt reply.

'Well . . .' began the policeman.

He was interrupted by a voice from outside the van, 'You're wanted here for a moment, Sergeant.'

With an order, 'Switch off your engine,' the policeman jumped out of the van to join his colleague. At that moment Alfie, in despair, hurled himself against the side of the crate and, scratching frantically, howled and howled.

'A refrigerator *howling*?' Alfie heard the policeman shout as he climbed back into the van. 'Let's see what you've really got in your van.'

The crate was unloaded on to the road. Alfie blinked when it was opened and he and Rex were revealed. He noticed first the two sullen men being held by police.

'Well, well, well,' said the first policeman. 'A

rocking-horse and a cat.' He lifted the railway cat out of the crate. 'How did you get in there?' he asked.

'Miaow!' said Alfie. Rex and I were being taken for a ride.

'Does he belong to you?' asked the policeman turning to the robbers.

'No!' snarled one, with a baleful glance at Alfie.

'Fancy being caught because of a stupid cat,' said the other man.

'A very clever cat, you should say,' said the police-

man. He stared at Alfie. 'I'm sure I've seen you before somewhere.'

Alfie purred. I've often been in the news, he wanted to tell him.

'We'll soon find out more about you, and the rocking-horse,' said the policeman.

Soon they were all at the police station. As Alfie lapped some milk he heard voices all around him, phones ringing and people coming and going. He enjoyed his time in police custody. He was given plenty to eat and drink and was congratulated time after time for alerting the police.

Alfie wasn't in the least worried about getting back home. He'd been lost before, and Fred had always managed to find him. Sure enough, after several long telephone calls, the officer in charge came across to Alfie, who was sitting on a counter contentedly watching everything going on.

'We've traced your owners,' said the officer. 'You're Alfie, the railway cat.'

'Miaow!' said Alfie. Of course I am.

'I should have recognized you immediately, as I've seen your picture in the papers and on television. We could certainly do with a clever cat like you at *our* station,' he said.

●

Other books about Alfie are: *The Railway Cat*, *The Railway Cat and Digby* and *The Railway Cat's Secret*.

OLGA TAKES CHARGE

MICHAEL BOND

Illustrated by Hans Helweg

'Wheeeeee!' That's the noise my friend Olga makes when she is excited or wants some attention from Karen Sawdust who looks after her. She is very spoilt and rather vain, and she is the only guinea-pig who has had three books written about her, but she certainly deserves them.

To begin with, she is a *real* guinea-pig and she, her children and grandchildren, have lived with the author for more than thirty years, and in all that time she's never stopped having adventures, or *pretending* to have them. For as well as being unusually handsome, she's a marvellous story-teller, even though her friends, Noel the cat, Fangio the hedgehog and Graham the tortoise, sometimes find it hard to believe that her ancestors really rescued a princess in a tower by sacrificing their tails, or that Olga herself saved the Sawdust people's house from burning down, and scared away the dreadful Surrey Puma.

One of her best stories is about how guinea-pigs learnt to fly. Here it is:

●

It was while Olga was looking out on it all through her bedroom window that she noticed something very strange. When she put her nose close to the glass and breathed out it became all misty so that she could no longer see through it. She tried it several times and each time added to the first, so that in the end it was just like the special glass the Sawdust family had in their bathroom.

In the end, tiring of this and feeling rather thirsty after all the effort, she went into her dining-room to have a drink, only to discover that her bowl of water had a coating of ice over the top.

'Wheeeeee!' She gave a shrill squeak, which said, in effect, 'Isn't it about time I was taken care of?'

The only effect it had on Noel was to make him stare lazily in her direction as much as to say, 'What's wrong now?'

'Wheeeeeeee!' said Olga. 'It's all very well for you. I expect you've had your breakfast, but I haven't. I'm hungry. Wheeeeeeeee!'

'You'll be lucky,' grunted Noel. 'It's Sunday. They're all still in bed.'

'In that case,' said Olga, 'I shall give a very loud squeak. I shall squeak so loud it will go into the house, through your pussy flap, through the kitchen, then the hall, up the stairs and into the bedrooms, and it will wake them all up, so there!' And she took a deep, deep breath, just to show what she meant.

'Huh!' said Noel unsympathetically. 'Pigs might fly.'

It was a phrase he'd heard the Sawdust family use several evenings before and he'd been waiting to try it out on Olga, knowing it might upset her – for she hated being called a pig.

Olga paused, let out her breath and stared at Noel. 'Would you mind saying that again?' she demanded.

'Pigs might fly,' said Noel carelessly. 'That means it's never likely to happen.'

'Never likely to happen!' repeated Olga. *'Never likely to happen!'* She was so upset her imagination went soaring up into the clouds in an effort to think of something, anything, to wipe the superior look off Noel's face. As it did so her sharp ears caught the sound of an aeroplane high above in the sky. Suddenly an idea came into her mind.

'I'll have you know,' she said, 'that guinea-pigs are some of the best flyers in the world. Much better than birds. They can go much, much higher for a start.'

Noel's jaw dropped. He was used to Olga's extravagant claims and her tall stories, but this one threatened to be the tallest and most extravagant ever. Even Graham and Fangio stopped in their tracks as they passed by on their way down the garden.

Graham, who'd been about to say goodnight for the winter, looked most impressed.

'I never knew that,' he said. 'I hope it doesn't keep me awake. I don't suppose it will.'

Noel gave a disparaging snort. 'I've never seen a pig flying,' he said. 'Nor's anyone else.'

'Not *pigs*,' said Olga. 'They'd be much too heavy. *Guinea*-pigs.

'Guinea-pigs,' she went on, 'are as light as a feather. They're really all fur. The lightest, softest, downiest fur imaginable. Why, they're so light they have to be tied down sometimes to keep them on the ground. A puff of wind and they're away.

'Not like cat's fur. That's very thick and heavy. Now, *there's* something that couldn't possibly fly. Not in a million years.'

Noel's snort was almost as loud as Olga's squeak might have been had she ever made it.

'Show me one,' he said. 'Just show me one.'

Olga glanced up towards the sky again. She was only just in time, for the aeroplane was almost out of sight.

'There's one going over right now,' she said.

Her remark was greeted in silence.

'That's not a guinea-pig,' said Noel at last.

'It is,' said Olga firmly.

'How do you know it is?' said Noel. 'Prove it.'

'How do you know it *isn't*?' asked Olga, conscious of playing a trump card. 'You prove it isn't.'

For once Noel was stuck for an answer.

'If you can fly,' he said at last, 'why don't you? If you're so good at it, show us. You can't even jog, let alone fly.'

'Where are your wings?' piped up Fangio. 'I can't see them.'

'I keep them tucked away,' said Olga primly.

'Anyway,' she turned and stared pityingly at Noel, 'I couldn't possibly fly in here. I'd only bang my head on the roof. Besides, I'm a bit out of practice. That's the trouble with being stuck in a cage all day. It makes you stiff.'

'I wonder where it was going?' said Graham, who'd

nearly ricked his neck trying to follow the progress of the plane.

'Probably somewhere warm for the winter,' said Fangio. 'That's what a lot of birds do.'

'Quite largely,' said Olga, glad that at least two members of her audience were on her side at last.

'Well, I still don't believe it,' said Noel. 'You might just as well say that was a tortoise,' he added, as a motor cycle roared past outside.

'If you think *that* you'll think anything,' said Olga. 'Besides, it was going much too fast.

'The thing is,' she continued, 'it all began many, many years ago, long before any of us were born, in the days when guinea-pigs lived in caves.

'That's why we're called "cavies", you know — because we once lived in caves.'

'That's true,' said Graham. 'I've heard that.'

'I live in a garage,' said Fangio, 'but I'm not called a "garages".'

Olga ignored the interruption. It really wasn't worth replying to.

'Some of you,' she went on, looking pointedly towards Noel, '*may* be able to picture what it must have been like all those years ago when they first saw daylight. Picture living in a big cave all your life, in the dark, and then suddenly one day finding the way out into the daylight.

'They were so excited they jumped for joy and to their astonishment they found themselves floating.

And because they were so light and because they were already high up, for the cave was at the top of a high mountain, they floated away, way up into the sky.

'That's how they ended up in so many different parts of the world. I expect my ancestors landed in the pet shop down the road and that's how I came to be here.'

Olga settled back, well pleased with her tale. Once she'd got going it had all fallen into place very nicely indeed.

As she did so another aeroplane, going very fast this time, and much lower, shot by. Fortunately, it was on the other side of the house and out of sight.

'There goes another one,' she said. 'It sounded as if it was in a hurry to get somewhere. I expect it's going off to do a good deed. Guinea-pigs are always doing good deeds somewhere or other, you know.'

Noel made a choking sound.

'Is something the matter?' asked Olga innocently.

Noel glared up at the sky where a distant drone and a long vapour trail showed where yet another plane was passing overhead. 'You'll be saying next they blow steam out of their noses like those dragons you told us about once.'

'I'm very glad you mentioned that,' said Olga. 'They're what's known as guinea-pig trails. Every time you see them it means there's a guinea-pig going somewhere.

'If you hadn't mentioned it I might have forgotten to tell you. You see, I may not be able to fly myself any more, but that's one thing I *can* still do — make trails.'

And so saying, she hurried into her bedroom, took up her position behind the window, drew in the deepest breath she could manage, and blew out as hard as she could.

'Well I never!' said Graham, as Olga's window went misty. 'Would you believe it?'

'*I* wouldn't have,' said Fangio. 'But I do now.'

Olga hurried out into her dining-room. 'How about you?' she called to Noel. 'Do you believe it now?' But Noel was already disappearing over the fence. He'd seen a squirrel and that was much more interesting.

'Goodnight,' said Graham. 'I shall sleep well after that.'

'Hear! Hear!' agreed Fangio. 'See you next spring.'

'Goodnight,' said Olga. She gazed after the other two as they went on their way. 'If you have any trouble getting to sleep, try counting guinea-pigs,' she called. 'They go over every day. I think I can hear another one coming now.'

'Oh, we shan't,' came a sleepy voice, barely recognizable as Graham's. 'Not after that. Stories make you sleepy.'

With that remark Olga agreed wholeheartedly. In fact, she went straight back into her bedroom and closed her eyes. Within moments she was fast asleep. But not for the winter, only until it was time for Sunday morning breakfast and another day.

●

This is an adventure from *Olga Takes Charge* and you'll find others in *Olga Carries On* and *The Tales of Olga da Polga*.

MILLY-MOLLY-MANDY STORIES

JOYCE LANKESTER BRISLEY

Illustrated by the Author

It's important to remember that the stories about Milly-Molly-Mandy were written seventy-seven years ago, when a penny was worth as much as a 50-pence piece today and it would buy 12 aniseed balls or a packet of safety pins or a skein of wool.

Milly-Molly-Mandy (whose real name was Millicent Margaret Amanda) lived with her Father and Mother, her Grandma and Grandpa *and* her Auntie and Uncle in a nice white cottage quite near to the village High Street, so that she was often kept quite busy running errands for them. At the beginning of this book there is a map which shows exactly where everything in the village is: like the blackberry patch (which had a notice saying 'Trespassers will be Prosecuted'), the meadow (where Milly and Billy practised the three-legged race), the Blacksmith's Forge and Miss Muggins' Shop, which Milly once looked after all by herself. Here she is, learning how to do it:

•

And then Milly-Molly-Mandy and little-friend-Susan, with their arms round each other, walked up the white road with the fields each side till they came to the Moggs' cottage, and little-friend-Susan

said 'Good-bye' and went in.

And Milly-Molly-Mandy went hoppity-skipping on alone till she came to the nice white cottage with the thatched roof, where Mother was at the gate to meet her.

Next day was Saturday, and Milly-Molly-Mandy went down to the village on an errand for Mother. And when she had done it she saw Miss Muggins standing at her shop door, looking rather worried.

And when Miss Muggins saw Milly-Molly-Mandy she said, 'Oh, Milly-Molly-Mandy, would you mind running to ask Mrs Jakes if she could come and mind my shop for an hour? Tell her I've got to go to see someone on very important business, and I don't know what to do, and Jilly's gone picnicking.'

So Milly-Molly-Mandy ran to ask Mrs Jakes. But Mrs Jakes said, 'Tell Miss Muggins I'm very sorry, but I've just got the cakes in the oven, and I can't leave them.'

So Milly-Molly-Mandy ran back and told Miss Muggins, and Miss Muggins said, 'I wonder if Mrs Blunt would come.'

So Milly-Molly-Mandy ran to ask Mrs Blunt. But Mrs Blunt said, 'I'm sorry, but I'm simply up to my eyes in house-cleaning, and I can't leave just now.'

So Milly-Molly-Mandy ran back and told Miss Muggins, and Miss Muggins said she didn't know of anyone else she could ask.

Then Milly-Molly-Mandy said, 'Oh, Miss Muggins, couldn't I look after the shop for you? I'll tell people you'll be back in an hour, and if they only want a sugar-stick or something I could give it them – I know how much it is!'

Miss Muggins looked at Milly-Molly-Mandy, and then she said. 'Well, you aren't very big, but I know you're careful, Milly-Molly-Mandy.'

So she gave her lots of instructions about asking people if they would come back in an hour, and not selling things unless she was quite sure of the price, and so on. And then Miss Muggins put on her hat and feather boa and hurried off.

And Milly-Molly-Mandy was left alone in charge of the shop!

Milly-Molly-Mandy felt very solemn and careful indeed. She dusted the counter with a duster which she saw hanging on a nail; and then she peeped into the window at all the handkerchiefs and socks and bottles of sweets – and she could see Mrs Hubble arranging the loaves and cakes in her shop window opposite, and Mr Smale (who had the grocer's shop with a little counter at the back where you posted parcels and bought stamps and letter-paper) standing at his door enjoying the sunshine. And Milly-Molly-Mandy felt so pleased that she had a shop as well as they.

And then, suddenly, the door-handle rattled, and the little bell over the door jangle-jangled up and down, and who should come in but little-friend-Susan! – And how little-friend-Susan did stare when she saw Milly-Molly-Mandy behind the counter!

'Miss Muggins has gone out on 'portant business, but she'll be back in an hour. What do you want?' said Milly-Molly-Mandy.

'A packet of safety-pins for Mother. What are you doing here?' said little-friend-Susan.

'I'm looking after the shop,' said Milly-Molly-Mandy. 'And I know where the safety-pins are, because I had to buy some yesterday.'

So Milly-Molly-Mandy wrapped up the safety-pins in a piece of thin brown paper, and twisted the end just as Miss Muggins did. And she handed the packet to little-friend-Susan, and little-friend-Susan handed her a penny.

And then little-friend-Susan wanted to stay and play 'shops' with Milly-Molly-Mandy.

But Milly-Molly-Mandy shook her head solemnly and said, 'No, this isn't play; it's business. I've got to be very, very careful. You'd better go, Susan.'

And just then the bell jangled again, and a lady came in, so little-friend-Susan went out. (She peered through the window for a time to see how Milly-Molly-Mandy got on, but Milly-Molly-Mandy wouldn't look at her.)

The lady was Miss Bloss, who lived opposite, over the baker's shop, with Mrs Bloss. She wanted a quarter of a yard of pink flannelette, because she was making a wrapper for her mother, and she hadn't bought quite enough for the collar. She said she didn't like to waste a whole hour till Miss Muggins returned.

Milly-Molly-Mandy stood on one leg and wondered what to do, and Miss Bloss tapped with one finger and wondered what to do.

And then Miss Bloss said, 'That's the roll my flannelette came off. I'm quite sure Miss Muggins wouldn't mind my taking some.'

So between them they measured off the pink flannelette, and Milly-Molly-Mandy fetched Miss Muggins' big scissors, and Miss Bloss made a crease exactly where the quarter-yard came; and Milly-Molly-Mandy breathed very hard and cut slowly and carefully right along the crease to the end.

And then she wrapped the piece up and gave it to Miss Bloss, and Miss Bloss handed her half a crown, saying, 'Ask Miss Muggins to send me the change when she gets back.'

And then Miss Bloss went out.

And then for a time nobody came in, and Milly-Molly-Mandy amused herself by trying to find the rolls of stuff that different people's dresses had come off. There was her own pink-and-white-striped cotton (looking so lovely and new) and Mother's blue-checked apron stuff and Mrs Jakes' Sunday gown . . .

Then rattle went the handle and jangle went the bell, and who should come in but Billy Blunt!

'I'm Miss Muggins,' said Milly-Molly-Mandy. 'What do you want to buy?'

'Where's Miss Muggins?' said Billy Blunt.

So Milly-Molly-Mandy had to explain again. And then Billy Blunt said he had wanted a pennyworth of aniseed balls. So Milly-Molly-Mandy stood on a box and reached down the glass jar from the shelf.

They were twelve a penny she knew, for she had often bought them. So she counted them out, and then Billy Blunt counted them.

And Billy Blunt said, 'You've got one too many here.'

So Milly-Molly-Mandy counted again, and she found one too many too. So they dropped one back in the jar, and Milly-Molly-Mandy put the others into a little bag and swung it over by the corners, just as Miss Muggins did, and gave it to Billy Blunt. And Billy Blunt gave her his penny.

And then Billy Blunt grinned, and said, 'Good morning, ma'am.'

And Milly-Molly-Mandy said, 'Good morning, sir,' and Billy Blunt went out.

After that an hour began to seem rather a long time, with the sun shining so outside. But at last the little bell gave a lively jangle again, and Miss Muggins had returned!

And though Milly-Molly-Mandy had enjoyed herself very much, she thought perhaps, after all, she would rather wait until she was grown up before she kept a shop for herself.

●

There are three other books about Milly-Molly-Mandy. They are *Further Doings of Milly-Molly-Mandy*, *More of Milly-Molly-Mandy* and *Milly-Molly-Mandy Again*.

MR MAJEIKA

HUMPHREY CARPENTER

Illustrated by Frank Rodgers

It's not very often that a new teacher arrives at school on a magic carpet, but Class Three at St Barty's Primary thought it was a fine idea, especially when the awful Hamish Bigmore was so exasperating that Mr Majeika forgot to be an ordinary teacher and said a few magic words or pointed a magic finger. (That's how Hamish got vampire's teeth and how, another time, he turned into a frog and had to live in the tadpole bowl for three days.) Yes, Class Three had a lovely time with their ex-wizard teacher, and you will too!

●

For a long time after that Mr Magic, as all Class Three were soon calling him, *didn't* forget that he was meant to be a teacher, and not a wizard. Nothing peculiar happened for weeks and weeks, and the lessons went on just as they would have with any other teacher. The magic carpet, the chips, and the snake seemed like a dream.

Then Hamish Bigmore came to stay at Thomas and Pete's house.

This wasn't at all a good thing, at least not for

Thomas and Pete. But they had no choice. Hamish Bigmore's mother and father had to go away for a few days, and Thomas and Pete's mum had offered to look after Hamish until they came back. She never asked Thomas and Pete what they thought about the idea until it was too late.

Hamish Bigmore behaved even worse than they had expected. He found all their favourite books and games, which they had tried to hide from him, and spoilt them or left them lying about the house where they got trodden on and broken. He pulled the stuffing out of Wim's favourite teddy bear, bounced up and down so hard on the garden climbing-frame that it bent, and talked for hours and hours after the light had been put out at night, so that Thomas and Pete couldn't get to sleep. 'It's awful,' said Thomas. 'I wish that something really nasty would happen to him.'

And it did.

Hamish Bigmore was behaving just as badly at school as at Thomas and Pete's house. The business of the ruler turning into a snake had frightened him for a few days, but no longer than that, and now he was up

47

to his old tricks again, doing anything rather than listen to Mr Majeika and behave properly.

On the Wednesday morning before Hamish Bigmore's mother and father were due to come home, Mr Majeika was giving Class Three a nature-study lesson, with the tadpoles in the glass tank that sat by his desk. Hamish Bigmore was being ruder than ever.

'Does anyone know how long tadpoles take to turn into frogs?' Mr Majeika asked Class Three.

'Haven't the slightest idea,' said Hamish Bigmore.

'Please,' said Melanie, holding up her hand, 'I don't think it's very long. Only a few weeks.'

'*You* should know,' sneered Hamish Bigmore. 'You look just like a tadpole yourself.'

Melanie began to cry.

'Be quiet, Hamish Bigmore,' said Mr Majeika. 'Melanie is quite right. It all happens very quickly. The tadpoles grow arms and legs, and very soon –'

'I shouldn't think they'll grow at all if they see *you* staring in at them through the glass,' said Hamish Bigmore to Mr Majeika. 'Your face would frighten them to death!'

'Hamish Bigmore, I have had enough of you,' said

Mr Majeika. 'Will you stop behaving like this?'

'No, I won't!' said Hamish Bigmore.

Mr Majeika pointed a finger at him.

And Hamish Bigmore vanished.

There was complete silence. Class Three stared at the empty space where Hamish Bigmore had been sitting.

Then Pandora Green pointed at the glass tank, and began to shout: 'Look! Look! A frog! A frog! One of the tadpoles has turned into a frog!'

Mr Majeika looked closely at the tank. Then he put his head in his hands. He seemed very upset.

'No, Pandora,' he said. 'It isn't one of the tadpoles. It's Hamish Bigmore.'

For a moment, Class Three were struck dumb. Then everyone burst out laughing. 'Hooray! Hooray! Hamish Bigmore has been turned into a frog! Good old Mr Magic!'

'It looks like Hamish Bigmore, doesn't it?' Pete said to Thomas. Certainly the frog's expression looked very much like Hamish's face. And it was splashing noisily around the tank and carrying on in the silly sort of way that Hamish did.

Mr Majeika looked very worried. 'Oh dear, oh dear,' he kept saying.

'Didn't you mean to do it?' said Jody.

Mr Majeika shook his head. 'Certainly not. I quite forgot myself. It was a complete mistake.'

'Well,' said Thomas, 'you can turn him back again, can't you?'

Mr Majeika shook his head again. 'I'm not at all sure that I can,' he said.

Thomas and Pete looked at him in astonishment.

'You see,' he went on, 'it was an old spell, something I learnt years and years ago and thought I'd forgotten. I don't know what were the exact words I used. And, as I am sure you understand, it's not possible to undo a spell unless you know exactly what the words were.'

'So Hamish Bigmore may have to stay a frog?' said Pete. 'That's the best thing I've heard for ages!'

Mr Majeika shook his head. 'For you, maybe, but not for him. I'll have to try and do *something*.' And he began to mutter a whole series of strange-sounding words under his breath.

All kinds of things began to happen. The room went dark, and the floor seemed to rock. Green smoke came out of an empty jar on Mr Majeika's desk. He tried some more words, and this time there was a small thunderstorm in the sky outside. But nothing happened to the frog.

'Oh, dear,' sighed Mr Majeika, 'what *am* I going to do?'

●

Mr Majeika appears in several books. They are *Mr Majeika, Mr Majeika and the Dinner Lady, Mr Majeika and the Haunted Hotel, Mr Majeika and the Music Teacher* and *Mr Majeika and the School Play.*

RAMONA AND HER MOTHER

BEVERLY CLEARY

Illustrated by Alan Tiegreen

Some readers may think that Ramona is a bit too young to have as a friend, but she is so funny and full of life that you'll soon want to read every single story about her and her friendly enemy, Howie, not to mention her elder sister Beezus (Beatrice). And, of course, she is growing up all the time — although she never stops getting into trouble, or making mistakes, however hard she tries. In the first story about her she is just starting school, but by the end of the series of books she's nearly three years older. The other good thing about Ramona is that she has such nice parents: Mr Quimby is sometimes out of a job so her mother has to go out to work, but they always take trouble over their children. In this story, Ramona feels cross when she has to look after silly little Willa Jean instead of joining the party.

•

Mrs Quimby, assisted by Beezus, set out a platter of scrambled eggs and another of bacon and sausage beside the gelatine salad. Hastily she snatched two small plates from the cupboard and dished out two servings of brunch, which she set in front of Ramona and Willa Jean. Beezus, acting like a grown-up, filled a basket with muffins and carried it into the dining room. Guests took plates from the stack at the end of the table and began to serve themselves.

Ramona scowled. If Beezus got to eat in the living room with the grown-ups, why couldn't she? She was no baby. She would not spill.

'Be a good girl!' whispered Mrs Quimby, who had forgotten the marmalade.

I'm trying, thought Ramona, but her mother was too flurried to notice her efforts. Willa Jean took one bite of scrambled eggs and then went to work, patting the rest flat on her plate with the back of her spoon.

Ramona watched her charge give her egg a final pat with the back of her spoon, pick up her bear, and trot off to the living room, leaving Ramona alone to nibble a muffin, think, and look at her artwork, arithmetic papers, and some cartoons her father had drawn, which had been taped to the refrigerator door for the family to admire. Nobody missed Ramona, all alone out there in the kitchen. Conversation from the living room was boring, all about high prices and who would be the next president, with no mention of children or anything interesting until someone said, 'Oops. Careful, Willa Jean.'

Then Mrs Kemp said, 'No-no, Willa Jean. Mustn't put your fingers in Mr Grumbie's marmalade. It's sticky.'

Mrs Quimby slipped into the kitchen to see if the coffee was ready. 'Ramona, it's time to take Willa Jean to your room and give her your present,' she whispered.

'I changed my mind,' said Ramona.

Mr Quimby, refilling the muffin basket, overheard. 'Do as your mother says,' he ordered in a whisper, 'so that kid will give us a little peace.'

Ramona considered. Should she make a fuss? What would a fuss accomplish? On the other hand, if she gave Willa Jean her present, maybe she would have a chance to hold that lovable bear for a little while.

'OK,' Ramona agreed without enthusiasm.

Mrs Quimby followed Ramona into the living room. 'Willa Jean,' she said. 'Ramona has a present for you. In her room.'

Willa Jean's attention was caught.

'Go with Ramona,' Mrs Quimby said firmly.

Willa Jean, still clutching her bear, went.

'Here.' Ramona thrust the package at Willa Jean, and when her guest set her bear on the bed, Ramona started to pick him up.

Willa Jean dropped the package. 'Woger's my bear,' she said, and ran off to the living room with him. In a moment she returned bearless to pull and yank and tear the wrapping from the package. 'That's not a present.' Willa Jean looked cross. 'That's Kleenex.'

'But it's your very own,' said Ramona. 'Sit down and I'll show you what to do.' She broke the perforation in the top of the box and pulled out one pink sheet and then another. 'See. You can sit here and pull out all you want because it's your very own. You can pull out the whole box if you want.' She did not bother telling Willa Jean that she had always wanted to pull out a whole box of Kleenex, one sheet after another.

Willa Jean looked interested. Slowly she pulled out one sheet and then a second. And another and another. She began to pull faster. Soon she was pulling out sheet after sheet and having such a good time that Ramona wanted to join the fun.

'It's mine,' said Willa Jean when Ramona reached for a tissue. Willa Jean got to her feet and, pulling and flinging, ran down the hall to the living room. Ramona followed.

'See me!' Willa Jean ordered the grown-ups as she ran around pulling and flinging Kleenex all over the room. Guests grabbed their coffee mugs and held them high for safety.

'No-no, Willa Jean,' said Mrs Kemp. 'Mrs Quimby won't like you wasting her Kleenex.'

'It's mine!' Willa Jean was carried away by the joy of wasting Kleenex and being the centre of attention at the same time. 'Ramona gave it to me.'

Ramona looked around for the bear, which was sitting on Mr Grumbie's lap. 'Would you like me to hold Roger?' Ramona asked, careful not to say Woger.

'No.' The bear's owner saw through Ramona's scheme. 'Woger wants to sit *there*.' Mr Grumbie did not look particularly pleased.

Willa Jean's parents made no effort to stop their daughter's spree of pull and fling. Ramona watched, feeling much older than she had earlier in the day. She also felt awkward while Beezus moved around the living room, dodging Willa Jean and pouring coffee as if she were a grown-up herself.

At first guests were amused by Willa Jean. But amusement faded as coffee mugs had to be rescued every time Willa Jean passed by. Pink Kleenex littered the room. Ramona heard Mr Huggins whisper, 'How much Kleenex in a box anyway?'

Mrs McCarthy answered, 'Two hundred and fifty sheets.'

'That's a lot of Kleenex,' said Mr Huggins.

When Willa Jean came to the last piece of Kleenex, she climbed on the couch and carefully laid it on Mr Grumbie's bald head. 'Now you have a hat,' she said.

Conversation died, and the party died, too. No one called Willa Jean an angel now or blessed her little heart.

The Grumbies were first to leave. Mr Grumbie handed the bear to Willa Jean's mother as Willa Jean filled her arms with pink tissues and tossed them into the air. 'Whee!' she cried, and scooped up another armful. 'Whee!'

Their departure seemed to be a signal for everyone to leave. 'Don't you want to take the Kleenex with you?' Mrs Quimby asked Willa Jean's mother. 'We can put it in a bag.'

'That's all right. Willa Jean has had her fun.' Mrs Kemp was helping Willa Jean into her coat.

'Bye-bye,' said Willa Jean prettily as her father carried her and Woger out the door.

Other guests were telling Mr and Mrs Quimby how much they had enjoyed the brunch. Beezus was standing beside them as if it had been her party, too. Mrs McCarthy smiled. 'I can see you are your mother's girl,' she said.

'I couldn't get along without her,' Mrs Quimby replied generously.

'Goodbye, Juanita,' said little Mrs Swink.

'Goodbye, Mrs Swink,' answered Ramona, polite to the end.

She tossed an armful of Kleenex into the air so that her mother might notice her, too. Somehow tossing someone else's pulled-out Kleenex was not much fun, and Mrs Quimby was so busy saying goodbye to other guests she did not pay attention.

At last the door was closed, and from the porch where the neighbours were opening umbrellas, Ramona's sharp ears caught her name. 'Willa Jean certainly reminds me of Ramona when she was Willa Jean's age,' someone said.

And someone else answered, 'She's Ramona all over again, all right.'

Ramona was filled with indignation. Willa Jean is *not* me all over again, she thought fiercely. I was never such a pest.

'Whew!' said Mr Quimby. 'That's over. What's the matter with those people, letting the kid show off like that?'

'Too much grandmother, I suppose,' answered Mrs Quimby. 'Or maybe it's easier for them to ignore her behaviour.'

'Come on, let's all pitch in and clean up this place,' said Mrs Quimby. 'Ramona, you find a bag and pick up all the Kleenex.'

'Kleenex is made of trees,' said Beezus, already helping her mother collect coffee mugs from the living room. 'We shouldn't waste it.' Lately Beezus had become a friend of trees.

'Put the bag of Kleenex in the cupboard in the bathroom,' said Mrs Quimby, 'and let's all remember to use it.'

I never was as awful as Willa Jean, Ramona told herself as she went to work collecting two hundred and fifty pieces of scattered pink Kleenex. I just know I wasn't. She followed the trail of Kleenex back to her bedroom, and when the two hundred and fiftieth piece was stuffed in the bag, she leaned against her dresser to study herself in the mirror.

How come nobody ever calls me my mother's girl? Ramona thought. How come Mother never says she couldn't get along without me?

•

Ramona and her sister feature in seven books. These are: *Beezus and Ramona, Ramona and Her Father, Ramona and Her Mother, Ramona Quimby, Age 8, Ramona the Brave, Ramona the Pest* and *Ramona Forever*.

FANTASTIC MR FOX

ROALD DAHL

Illustrated by Jill Bennett

Stories about Foxes are almost always stories about Food, and how cunning and clever they are at finding it. This Mr Fox needs to be particularly clever because he has three particularly awful enemies. They are rich farmers, and 'as nasty and mean as any men you could meet'. Farmer Boggis keeps thousands of chickens and is very fat. Farmer Bunce, who is very short, breeds ducks and geese and lives on doughnuts and goose liver, and Farmer Bean, who is as thin as a pencil, keeps turkeys and drinks his own cider. Of course, they all think Mr Fox is *their* enemy, and this story is about all the ways they try to catch him, and how he always escapes because — as Mrs Fox keeps telling their four children — 'Your father is a fantastic fox'. Here is a bit of the story:

•

*B*ack in the tunnel they paused so that Mr Fox could brick up the hole in the wall. He was humming to himself as he put the bricks back in place. 'I can still taste that glorious cider,' he said. 'What an impudent fellow Rat is.'

'He has bad manners,' Badger said. 'All rats have

bad manners. I've never met a polite rat yet.'

'And he drinks too much,' said Mr Fox, putting the last brick in place. 'There we are. Now, home to the feast!'

They grabbed their jars of cider and off they went. Mr Fox was in front, the Smallest Fox came next and Badger last. Along the tunnel they flew ... past the turning that led to Bunce's Mighty Storehouse ... past Boggis's Chicken-House Number One and then up the long home stretch toward the place where they knew Mrs Fox would be waiting.

'Keep it up, my darlings!' shouted Mr Fox. 'We'll soon be there! Think what's waiting for us at the other end! And just think what we're bringing home with us in these jars! That ought to cheer up poor Mrs Fox.' Mr Fox sang a little song as he ran:

> 'Home again swiftly I glide,
> Back to my beautiful bride.
> She'll not feel so rotten
> As soon as she's gotten
> Some cider inside her inside.'

Then Badger joined in:

> 'Oh poor Mrs Badger, he cried,
> So hungry she very near died.
> But she'll not feel so hollow
> If only she'll swallow
> Some cider inside her inside.'

They were still singing as they rounded the final corner and burst in upon the most wonderful and amazing sight any of them had ever seen. The feast was just beginning. A large dining-room had been hollowed out of the earth, and in the middle of it, seated around a huge table, were no less than twenty-nine animals. They were:

Mrs Fox and three Small Foxes.

Mrs Badger and three Small Badgers.

Mole and Mrs Mole and four Small Moles.

Rabbit and Mrs Rabbit and five Small Rabbits.

Weasel and Mrs Weasel and six Small Weasels.

The table was covered with chickens and ducks and geese and hams and bacon, and everyone was tucking into the lovely food.

'My darling!' cried Mrs Fox, jumping up and hugging Mr Fox. 'We couldn't wait! Please forgive us!' Then she hugged the Smallest Fox of all, and Mrs Badger hugged Badger, and everyone hugged everyone else. Amid shouts of joy, the great jars of cider were placed upon the table, and Mr Fox and Badger and the Smallest Fox sat down with the others.

You must remember no one had eaten a thing for several days. They were ravenous. So for a while there was no conversation at all. There was only the sound of crunching and chewing as the animals attacked the succulent food.

At last, Badger stood up. He raised his glass of cider and called out, 'A toast! I want you all to stand and drink a toast to our dear friend who has saved our lives this day – Mr Fox!'

'To Mr Fox!' they all shouted, standing up and raising their glasses. 'To Mr Fox! Long may he live!'

Then Mrs Fox got shyly to her feet and said, 'I don't want to make a speech. I just want to say one thing, and it is this: MY HUSBAND IS A FANTAS-TIC FOX.' Everyone clapped and cheered.

TOTTIE: The Story of a Dolls' House

RUMER GODDEN

Here's a story about a doll whom you will never forget, because she is so kind and brave. Tottie is very tiny and made of wood. She lives with three other dolls: Mr Plantaganet, his wife Birdie who is made of celluloid, their little boy Apple, and a dog, called Darner because he is made out of a pipe cleaner and a darning needle.

They are all quite happy, though they long for a home of their own instead of the old shoe box they live in — then one day their children, Emily and Charlotte, are given an old dolls' house, and they think they'll be happy ever after, until a bad selfish doll called Marchpane is sent to live with them. She ruins everything by spoiling Apple and treating all the others as servants. All they can do is wish very hard and at last it turns out all right. But before that happens Tottie has a different adventure: she is sent to an Exhibition where the Queen wants to buy her — and alas, Marchpane is there.

•

The Exhibition was almost over. Many people had visited it; it was a great success.

Most of the people had taken notice of Tottie. 'What a little love of a doll,' they had said. 'But that is what they say about Apple,' said Tottie. 'Oh, Apple. I long to see you again.'

Emily and Charlotte had been several times to visit her. 'Dear possession,' thought Tottie, 'a great treasure.' That was what Mrs Innisfree and the Queen had said. Tottie could look them in the face now, happily. 'She doesn't look hurt any more,' said Emily.

'And we never found out why she did,' said Charlotte. 'That is the worst of dolls. They are such secret people.'

They showed Tottie a cutting from a newspaper. It gave an account of the Exhibition: '. . . *and the smallest doll is a hundred-year-old farthing doll, lent by Emily and Charlotte Dane.*' If anyone had listened, they might have heard a tiny gritting sound. It was Marchpane grinding her china teeth.

Emily and Charlotte had looked at Marchpane and admired her very much, especially Emily; they knew she had belonged to Great-Great-Aunt Laura, but they did not know she had lived with Tottie in the dolls' house.

Tottie was longing to go home, but the other dolls were, for the most part, sorry the Exhibition was over. They would be packed away again or sent back to their museums.

'What is a museum like?' asked Tottie.

'It is cold dere,' said the walking doll suddenly. She sounded quite unlike herself.

'Nonsense. It is grand and fine,' said Marchpane. 'It

is filled with precious and valuable things kept in glass cases.'

'I shouldn't enjoy that,' said Tottie, looking at Queen Victoria's dolls. 'How can you be played with if you are in a glass case?'

'One wouldn't want to be played with,' said Marchpane. 'When I was at the cleaners, people said I ought to be in a museum.'

'It is cold dere,' said the walking doll again.

'It is grand and fine,' said Marchpane.

'*C'est vrai mais —*' said the walking doll. '*Mais —*' Her voice sounded as if her works had quite run down.

'I don't want to go back in my box,' said the wax doll. 'It is too dark and quiet. I wish . . .' She was thinking of the caretaker's child who still crept out to look at her in the evenings when the people had gone. 'I wish . . .'

The last day came. Tottie, with every minute, grew more happy and excited.

'You are lucky,' sighed the wax doll.

'Tell us about dis 'ouse you are in,' said the walking doll.

'Yes, tell us. Then I can think about it when I lie with my eyes shut in my box. I can think and pretend. Tell, Tottie. Tell us.'

All the dolls took up the cry. 'Tell us, Tottie. Tell.'

Tottie had always thought it better not to talk about the house in front of Marchpane, but now she

was so excited and happy herself and so sorry for the
other dolls that she forgot to take care. She began to
tell about the dolls' house.

She told about its cream walls and the ivy and
Darner's kennel. She told about the red hall and the
sitting-room with the holly-green carpet and the
struggle to get the chairs (though she did not tell that
she had thought that she herself had been sold to get
them). She told about the rooms upstairs and the pink
and blue carpets and the bath with the taps, and she
told about Birdie and Mr Plantaganet and Darner and
Apple. She told it from the beginning to the end,
from the bottom to the top. When she had done,
there was a long silence, and then a-aahs and sighs
from the dolls.

'If only . . .'

'I wish . . .'

'It might have been . . .'

'I wish . . .'

'If only . . .'

'If only . . .'

'Oh, lucky, lucky Tottie!'

'Oh, Tottie, you are lucky!'

'Don't you believe her,' cried Marchpane in a loud
voice. 'That isn't her house. It's mine.'

All the dolls looked at Marchpane. Then they all
looked at Tottie.

'You stole it while I was at the cleaners.'

'It is in our nursery now,' said Tottie. 'It was sent

to us, as you were sent to the cleaners. It needed cleaning and taking care of,' said Tottie. 'We cleaned it and took care of it.'

'How dare you!' cried Marchpane. 'You think because the Queen noticed you, you can do anything. Wait and see. Wait and see,' cried Marchpane. 'I shall have that house back.'

'How can you?' asked Tottie. 'It's in our nursery.'

'Wait and see,' said Marchpane. 'Wait and see.'

The Exhibition was closed. The dolls had been taken away, the room was empty, and when the caretaker's child came in the evening there were only long blank tables where Tottie and Marchpane and Queen Victoria's dolls and the walking doll and the wax doll and the other dolls had been.

Did the caretaker's child think of the wax doll? And the wax doll, in her lonely box, think of the caretaker's child and of the finger that had touched her satin dress? Did the dolls think of Tottie's welcome home by Emily, Charlotte, Birdie, Mr Plantaganet, Apple, and Darner?

I think they did.

•

There are two more lovely stories about dolls by Rumer Godden. They are called *Miss Happiness and Miss Flower* and *Candy Floss and Impunity Jane*.

THE WIND IN THE WILLOWS

KENNETH GRAHAME

Illustrated by Margaret Gordon

This story, which was written nearly 100 years ago, is one everybody should read, because it's funny and it's about friendship.

There are four friends: Mole, Ratty, Badger and Toad. Mole is the youngest and rather timid. Ratty is clever and likes messing about in boats. Badger is wise and a bit bossy. Toad is kind and generous, but rather silly and extremely boastful, so the other three are always trying to make him behave — especially when he steals a car and ends up in prison. He manages to escape dressed up as a washerwoman and has more disgraceful adventures. In this part of the story they are planning to recapture Toad Hall, which has been invaded by the villainous Stoats and Weasels.

•

Such a tremendous noise was going on in the banqueting-hall that there was little danger of their being overheard. The Badger said, 'Now, boys, all together!' and the four of them put their shoulders to the trap-door and heaved it back. Hoisting each other up, they found themselves standing in the pantry, with only a door between them and the banqueting-hall, where their enemies were carousing.

The noise, as they emerged from the passage, was simply deafening. At last, as the cheering and hammering slowly subsided, a voice could be made out saying, 'Well, I do not propose to detain you much longer' – (great applause) – 'but before I resume my seat' – (renewed cheering) – 'I should like to say one word about our kind host, Mr Toad. We all know Toad!' – (great laughter) – '*Good* Toad, *modest* Toad, *honest* Toad!' – (shrieks of merriment).

'Only just let me get at him!' muttered Toad, grinding his teeth.

'Hold hard a minute!' said the Badger, restraining him with difficulty. 'Get ready, all of you!'

'– Let me sing you a little song,' went on the voice, 'which I have composed on the subject of Toad' – (prolonged applause).

Then the Chief Weasel – for it was he – began in a high, squeaky voice:

> Toad he went a-pleasuring
> Gaily down the street –

The Badger drew himself up, took a firm grip of his stick with both paws, glanced round at his comrades and cried:

'The hour is come! Follow me!'

And flung the door open wide.

My!

What a squealing and a squeaking and a screeching filled the air!

Well might the terrified weasels dive under the tables and spring madly up at the windows! Well

might the ferrets rush wildly for the fireplace and get hopelessly jammed in the chimney! Well might tables and chairs be upset, and glass and china be sent crashing on the floor, in the panic of that terrible moment when the four Heroes strode wrathfully into the room! The mighty Badger, his whiskers bristling, his great cudgel whistling through the air; Mole, black and grim, brandishing his stick and shouting his awful war-cry, 'A Mole! A Mole!'; Rat, desperate and determined, his belt bulging with weapons of every age and every variety; Toad, frenzied with excitement and injured pride, swollen to twice his ordinary size, leaping into the air and emitting Toad-whoops that chilled them to the marrow! 'Toad he went a-pleasuring!' he yelled. 'I'll pleasure 'em!' and he went straight for the Chief Weasel. They were but four in all, but to the panic-stricken weasels the hall seemed full of monstrous animals, grey, black, brown, and yellow, whooping and flourishing enormous cudgels; and they broke and fled with squeals of terror and dismay, this way and that, through the windows, up the chimney, anywhere to get out of reach of those terrible sticks.

The affair was soon over. Up and down, the whole length of the hall, strode the four friends, whacking with their sticks at every head that showed itself, and in five minutes the room was cleared. Through the broken windows the shrieks of terrified weasels escaping across the lawn were borne faintly to their ears; on the floor lay prostrate some dozen or so of the

enemy, on whom the Mole was busily engaged in fitting handcuffs. The Badger, resting from his labours, leant on his stick and wiped his honest brow.

'Mole,' he said, 'you're the best of fellows! Just cut along outside and look after those stoat-sentries. I've an idea that we shan't have much trouble from *them* tonight!'

THE SHRINKING OF TREEHORN

FLORENCE PARRY HEIDE

Illustrated by Edward Gorey

This is Treehorn – he is my favourite person – he doesn't talk much, but he reads quite a lot, especially the words on cornflake boxes, and he sends away for all the free games and puzzles. Perhaps it was one of those which made him start shrinking. At first he didn't mind much and nobody noticed but then he got smaller and smaller . . .

•

At dinner that night Treehorn's father said, 'Do sit up, Treehorn. I can hardly see your head.'

'I *am* sitting up,' said Treehorn. 'This is as far up as I come. I think I must be shrinking or something.'

'I'm sorry my cake didn't turn out very well,' said Treehorn's mother.

'It's very nice, dear,' said Treehorn's father politely.

By this time Treehorn could hardly see over the top of the table.

'Sit up, dear,' said Treehorn's mother.

'I *am* sitting up,' said Treehorn. 'It's just that I'm shrinking.'

'What, dear?' asked his mother.

'I'm shrinking. Getting smaller,' said Treehorn.

'If you want to pretend you're shrinking, that's all right,' said Treehorn's mother, 'as long as you don't do it at the table.'

'But I *am* shrinking,' said Treehorn.

'Don't argue with your mother, Treehorn,' said Treehorn's father.

'He does look a little smaller,' said Treehorn's mother, looking at Treehorn. 'Maybe he *is* shrinking.'

'Nobody shrinks,' said Treehorn's father.

'Well, I'm shrinking,' said Treehorn. 'Look at me.'

Treehorn's father looked at Treehorn.

'Why, you're shrinking,' said Treehorn's father. 'Look, Emily, Treehorn is shrinking. He's much smaller

than he used to be.'

'Oh, dear,' said Treehorn's mother. 'First it was the cake, and now it's this. Everything happens at once.'

'I *thought* I was shrinking,' said Treehorn, and he went into the den to turn on the television set.

●

So what do you think happens to Treehorn? Does he get so small that he disappears? Perhaps not, because there's another book about him called *Treehorn's Treasure*, so you will have the fun of reading them both.

FINN FAMILY MOOMINTROLL

TOVE JANSSON

Illustrated by the Author

If I were seven years old and told I must choose just one book to take away with me on holiday, or to school, or for a long journey, I would choose this one; because instead of having just one friend to enjoy, I'd have an entire family. As well as shy, plump little Moomintroll, Moominmamma, Moominpappa, Snufkin, Sniff and the Hemulen, there would even be a few interesting enemies, like the Hattifatteners and the Hobgoblin.

Moominhouse is in a forest in Finland, and everyone goes to sleep all through the winter, but when the spring comes everyone wakes up and starts having adventures. Here is the first of them:

●

*I*t certainly promised to be a fine day. Everywhere befuddled little creatures just woken from their long winter sleep poked about rediscovering old haunts, and busied themselves airing clothes, brushing out their moustaches and getting their houses ready for the spring.

Many were building new homes and I am afraid some were quarrelling. (You can wake up in a very bad temper after such a long sleep.)

The Spirits that haunted the trees sat combing their long hair, and on the north side of the tree trunks, baby mice dug tunnels amongst the snowflakes.

'Happy spring!' said an elderly Earth-Worm. 'And how was the winter with you?'

'Very nice, thank you,' said Moomintroll. 'Did you sleep well, sir?'

'Fine,' said the Worm. 'Remember me to your father and mother.'

So they walked on, talking to a lot of people in this way, but the higher up the hill they went the less people there were, and at last they only saw one or two mother mice sniffing around and spring-cleaning.

It was wet everywhere.

'Ugh — how nasty,' said Moomintroll, picking his way gingerly through the melting snow. 'So much snow is never good for a Moomin. Mother said so.' And he sneezed.

'Listen, Moomintroll,' said Snufkin. 'I have an idea. What about going to the top of the mountain and making a pile of stones to show that we were the first to get there?'

'Yes, let's,' said Sniff, and set off at once so as to get there before the others.

When they reached the top the March wind gambolled around them, and the blue distance lay at their feet. To the west was the sea; to the east the river looped round the Lonely Mountains; to the north the great forest spread its green carpet, and to the south the smoke rose from Moomintroll's chimney, for Moominmamma was cooking the breakfast. But Sniff saw none of these things because on the top of the mountain lay a hat — a tall, black hat.

'Someone has been here before!' he said.

Moomintroll picked up the hat and looked at it. 'It's a *rarey* hat,' he said. 'Perhaps it will fit you, Snufkin.'

'No, no,' said Snufkin, who loved his old green hat. 'It's much too new.'

'Perhaps Father would like it,' mused Moomintroll.

'Well, anyway we'll take it with us,' said Sniff. 'But now I want to go home — I'm dying for some breakfast, aren't you?'

'I should say I am,' said Snufkin.

And that was how they found the Hobgoblin's Hat and took it home with them, without guessing for one moment that this would cast a spell on the Valley of the Moomins, and that before long they would all see strange things . . .

When Moomintroll, Snufkin, and Sniff went out on to the veranda the others had already had their breakfast and gone off in various directions. Moominpappa was alone reading the newspaper. 'Well, well! So you have woken up, too,' he said. 'Remarkably little in the paper today. A stream burst its dam and swamped a lot of ants. All saved. The first cuckoo arrived in the

valley at four o'clock and then flew off to the east.'
(This is a good omen, but a cuckoo flying west is still
better . . .)

'Look what we've found,' interrupted Moomintroll,
proudly. 'A beautiful new top hat for you!'

Moominpappa put aside his paper and examined the
hat very thoroughly. Then he put it on in front of the
long mirror. It was rather too big for him — in fact it
nearly covered his eyes, and the effect was very curious.

'Mother,' screamed Moomintroll. 'Come and look
at Father.'

Moominmamma opened the kitchen door and
looked at him with amazement.

'How do I look?' asked Moominpappa.

'It's all right,' said Moominmamma. 'Yes, you look very handsome in it, but it's just a tiny bit too big.'

'Is it better like this?' asked Moominpappa, pushing the hat on to the back of his head.

'Hm,' said Moominmamma. 'That's smart, too, but I almost think you look more dignified without a hat.'

Moominpappa looked at himself in front, behind and from both sides, and then he put the hat on the table with a sigh.

'You're right,' he said. 'Some people look better without hats.'

'Of course, dear,' said Moominmamma kindly. 'Now eat up your eggs, children, you need feeding up after living on pine needles all the winter.' And she disappeared into the kitchen again.

'But what shall we do with the hat?' asked Sniff. 'It's such a fine one.'

'Use it as a waste-paper basket,' said Moominpappa, and thereupon he took himself upstairs to go on writing his life story. (The heavy volume about his stormy youth.)

Snufkin put the hat down on the floor between the table and the kitchen door. 'Now you've got a new piece of furniture again,' he said, grinning, for Snufkin could never understand why people liked to *have* things. He was quite happy wearing the old suit he had had since he was born (nobody knows when and where that happened), and the only possession he didn't give away was his mouth-organ.

'If you've finished breakfast we'll go and see how the Snorks are getting on,' said Moomintroll. But before going out into the garden he threw his eggshell into the waste-paper basket, for he was (sometimes) a well brought up Moomin.

The dining-room was now empty.

In the corner between the table and the kitchen door stood the Hobgoblin's Hat with the eggshell in the bottom. And then something really strange happened. The eggshell began to change its shape.

(This is what happens, you see. If something lies long enough in the Hobgoblin's Hat it begins to change into something quite different — what that will be you never know beforehand. It was lucky that the hat hadn't fitted Moominpappa because the-Protector-of-all-Small-Beasts knows what would have come of him if he had worn it a bit longer. As it was he only got a slight headache — and that was over after dinner.)

Meanwhile the eggshell had become soft and woolly, although it still stayed white, and after a time it filled the hat completely. Then five small clouds broke away from the brim of the hat, sailed out on to the veranda, thudded softly down the steps and hung there just above the ground. The Hat was empty.

'Goodness gracious me,' said Moomintroll.

'Is the house on fire?' asked the Snork Maiden, anxiously.

The clouds were hanging in front of them without moving or changing shape, as if they were waiting for something, and the Snork Maiden put out her paw very cautiously and patted the nearest one. 'It feels like cotton wool,' she said, in a surprised voice. The others came near and felt it, too.

'Just like a little pillow,' said Sniff.

Snufkin gave one of the clouds a gentle push. It floated on a bit and then stopped again.

'Whose are they?' asked Sniff. 'How did they get on to the veranda?'

Moomintroll shook his head. 'It's the queerest thing I've ever come across,' he said. 'Perhaps we ought to go in and fetch Mother.'

'No, no,' said the Snork Maiden. 'We'll try them out ourselves,' and she dragged a cloud on to the ground and smoothed it out with her paw. 'So soft!'

said the Snork Maiden, and the next minute she was rocking up and down on the cloud with loud giggles.

'Can I have one, too?' squealed Sniff jumping on to another cloud. 'Hup-si-daisy!' But when he said 'hup' the cloud rose and made an elegant little curve over the ground.

'Golly!' burst out Sniff. 'It moved!'

Then they all threw themselves on to the clouds and shouted 'Hup! hup, hup-si-daisy.' The clouds bounded wildly about until the Snork discovered how to steer them. By pressing a little with one foot you could turn the cloud. If you pressed with both feet it went forward, and if you rocked gently the cloud slowed up.

They had terrific fun, even floating up to the tree-tops and to the roof of Moominhouse.

Moomintroll hovered outside Moominpappa's window and shouted: 'Cock-a-doodle-doo!' (He was so excited he couldn't think of anything more intelligent.)

Moominpappa dropped his memoir-pen and rushed to the window.

'Bless my tail!' he burst out. 'Whatever next!'

'It will make a good chapter for your story,' said Moomintroll, steering his cloud to the kitchen window where he shouted to his mother. But Moominmamma was in a great hurry and went on making rissoles. 'What have you found now, dear?' she said. 'Just be careful you don't fall down!'

But down in the garden the Snork Maiden and Snufkin had discovered a new game. They steered at each other at full speed and collided with a soft bump. Then the first to fall off had lost.

'Now we'll see!' cried Snufkin urging his cloud forward. But the Snork Maiden dodged cleverly to the side and then attacked him from underneath.

Snufkin's cloud capsized, and he fell on his head in the flower-bed and his hat fell over his eyes.

'Third round,' squeaked Sniff, who was referee and was flying a bit above the others. 'That's two : one! Ready, steady, go!'

'Shall we go on a little flying tour together?' Moomintroll asked the Snork Maiden.

'Certainly,' she answered, steering her cloud up beside his. 'Where shall we go?'

'Let's hunt up the Hemulen and surprise him,' suggested Moomintroll.

They made a tour of the garden, but the Hemulen wasn't in any of his usual haunts.

'He can't have gone far,' said the Snork Maiden. 'Last time I saw him he was sorting his stamps.'

'But that was six months ago,' said Moomintroll.

'Oh, so it was,' she agreed. 'We've slept since then, haven't we?'

'Did you sleep well, by the way?' asked Moomintroll.

The Snork Maiden flew elegantly over a tree-top and considered a little before answering. 'I had an awful dream,' she said at last. 'About a nasty man in a high, black hat who grinned at me.'

'How funny,' said Moomintroll. 'I had exactly the same dream. Had he got white gloves on, too?'

The Snork Maiden nodded, and slowly gliding through the forest they pondered on this awhile. Suddenly they caught sight of the Hemulen, who was wandering along with his hands behind his back and his eyes on the ground. Moomintroll and the Snork Maiden made perfect three-point landings on either side of him and called out brightly: 'Good morning!'

'Ouch! Oh!' gasped the Hemulen. 'How you frightened me! You shouldn't jump at me suddenly like that.'

'Oh, sorry,' said the Snork Maiden. 'Look what we're riding on.'

'That's most extraordinary,' said the Hemulen. 'But I'm so used to your doing extraordinary things that

nothing surprises me. Besides I'm feeling melancholy just now.'

'Why is that?' asked the Snork Maiden sympathetically. 'On such a fine day, too.'

'You wouldn't understand anyway,' said the Hemulen, shaking his head.

'We'll try,' said Moomintroll. 'Have you lost a rare stamp again?'

'On the contrary,' answered the Hemulen gloomily. 'I have them all: every single one. My stamp collection is complete. There is nothing missing.'

'Well, isn't that nice?' said the Snork Maiden, encouragingly.

'I said you'd never understand me, didn't I?' moaned the Hemulen.

Moomintroll looked anxiously at the Snork Maiden and they drew back their clouds a little out of consideration for the Hemulen's sorrow. He wandered on and they waited respectfully for him to unburden his soul.

At last he burst out:

'How hopeless it all is!' And after another pause he added: 'What's the use? You can have my stamp collection for the next paperchase.'

'But Hemulen!' said the Snork Maiden, horrified, 'that would be awful! Your stamp collection is the finest in the world!'

'That's just it,' said the Hemulen in despair. 'It's finished. There isn't a stamp, or an error, that I haven't collected. Not one. What shall I do now?'

'I think I'm beginning to understand,' said Moomintroll slowly. 'You aren't a collector any more, you're only an owner, and that isn't nearly so much fun.'

'No,' said the heartbroken Hemulen, 'not nearly.' He stopped and turned his puckered-up face towards them.

'Dear Hemulen,' said the Snork Maiden, taking him gently by the hand, 'I have an idea. What about your collecting something different — something quite new?'

'That's an idea,' admitted the Hemulen, but he continued to look worried because he thought he oughtn't to look happy after such a big sorrow.

'Butterflies for example?' suggested Moomintroll.

'Impossible,' said the Hemulen and became gloomy again. 'One of my second cousins collects them, and I can't stand him.'

'Film stars then?' said the Snork Maiden.

The Hemulen only sniffed.

'Ornaments?' Moomintroll said hopefully. 'They're never finished.'

But the Hemulen pooh-poohed that too.

'Well, then I really don't know,' said the Snork Maiden.

'We'll think of something for you,' said Moomintroll, consolingly. 'Mother's sure to know. By the way, have you seen the Muskrat?'

'He's still asleep,' the Hemulen answered sadly. 'He

says that it's unnecessary to get up so early, and I think he's right.' And with that he continued his lonely wanderings, while Moomintroll and the Snork Maiden steered their clouds right up over the tree-tops and rested there, rocking slowly in the sunshine. They considered the problem of the Hemulen's new collection.

'What about shells?' the Snork Maiden proposed.

'Or rarey buttons,' said Moomintroll.

But the warmth made them sleepy and didn't en-courage thinking, so they lay on their backs on the clouds and looked up at the spring sky where the larks were singing.

And suddenly they caught sight of the first butterfly. (As everyone knows, if the first butterfly you see is yellow the summer will be a happy one. If it is white then you will just have a quiet summer. Black and brown butterflies should never be talked about — they are much too sad.)

But this butterfly was golden.

'What can that mean?' said Moomintroll. 'I've never seen a golden butterfly before.'

'Gold is even better than yellow,' said the Snork Maiden. 'You wait and see!'

When they got home to dinner they met the Hemulen on the steps. He was beaming with happiness.

'Well?' said Moomintroll. 'What is it?'

'Nature study!' shouted the Hemulen. 'I shall bota-nize. The Snork thought of it. I shall collect the world's finest herbarium!' And the Hemulen spread out his skirt* to show them his first find. Among the earth and leaves lay a very small spring-onion.

'*Gagea lutea*,' said the Hemulen proudly. 'Number one in the collection. A perfect specimen.' And he went in and dumped the whole lot on the dining-table.

'Put it in the corner, Hemul dear,' said Moomin-mamma, 'because I want to put the soup there. Is everybody in? Is the Muskrat still sleeping?'

'Like a pig,' said Sniff.

'Have you had a good time today?' asked Moomin-mamma when she had filled all the plates.

'Wonderful,' cried the whole family.

Next morning when Moomintroll went to the wood-shed to let out the clouds they had all disappeared; every one of them. And nobody imagined that it had anything to do with the eggshell which was once again lying in the Hobgoblin's Hat.

●

There are seven more Moomin books, all as good as the first one. They are called *Comet in Moominland, The Exploits of Moominpappa, Moominland Midwinter, Moominpappa at Sea, Moominsummer Madness, Moominvalley in November* and *Tales from Moominvalley*.

* The Hemulen always wore a dress that he had inherited from his aunt. I believe all Hemulens wear dresses. It seems strange, but there you are. – Author's note.

ALBERT

ALISON JEZARD

Illustrated by Margaret Gordon

When it comes to making friends, Albert is better than anyone. It's because he's such a very polite bear, and so interested in everybody he meets. For instance, when the rag-and-bone man takes his old umbrella-stand by mistake, he makes friends with the horse and gets his stand back, as well as an umbrella to put in it.

And he's a very good housekeeper: his little basement in 14 Spoonbasher's Row is always polished and sparkling, he keeps a red geranium on the window-sill, he cooks his favourite sausages until they are crisp and brown, and most important, he never sits down to his tea without washing his paws first. In fact, wherever Albert goes he manages to have a lovely time. Among the things he does is helping the fire brigade, being a Christmas postman, and making hay on his friend's farm. But one day he will always remember is when he went with his cousin Angus to a football match . . .

•

Albert had brought in some fish and chips for lunch, because he thought he would like to give his cousin from Scotland something very English, but Angus told him they often had it at home, and it was really his favourite food, but Albert was not to tell Aunt Bertha that, because she would think that he ought to like haggis best.

The two bears had a good gossip about all they had been doing and ate their fish and chips in front of the fire out of the paper, as they both agreed that this was the way they tasted best and then Albert said it was time they set off for the football ground.

They went by tube train because Angus had never seen one. He was a little bit scared and hung on to Albert as they went down the moving staircase, but, by the time they reached their station, he had quite recovered and wanted to go up and down the es-calator again, but there wasn't time and Albert promised they would go home the same way.

They arrived at the ground and found their seats, which they were very pleased to see were right at the front and beside the passage where the players came out!

The two of them looked happily round and Angus said he thought the only better seats in the whole place would be in the directors' box!

Just as they sat down a band came marching out on to the pitch and began to play music for community singing. Albert and Angus sang as loudly as anyone and thoroughly enjoyed it, especially when they played 'Loch Lomond'.

When it was time for the kick-off, it was very exciting to watch the two teams running out from just beside them and forming up into two lines facing each other on the pitch. There they stood and nothing happened!

After a few minutes, as the players began to look at each other, a man came out and spoke to the two captains and the crowd watched as the three men looked round them and then the captain of the English team pointed and it seemed as if he were pointing straight at Albert! He was! The third man suddenly left the other two and came over to Albert and said, 'Excuse me, I am the manager of the English team. The Duke has sent a message to say that he is held up by a traffic block and he wants us to carry on without him. Would you care to kick off for us?'

Albert's mouth fell open. No words would come.

Then he felt Angus nudging him and saying, 'Of course he will kick off for you. He'll be very glad to –

won't you, Albert?' Now Angus was pushing him out of his seat and into the gangway. 'And I'll come with him,' he added.

And Albert was out on the pitch, with his mouth still open and Angus by his side, chatting happily with the manager.

Albert managed to close his mouth again while he was introduced to the Scottish team and Angus was introduced to the English team, but it was not until he was set in front of the ball that he gasped out, 'I've never kicked a ball!'

'Never mind,' answered the manager, 'all we need is for you to get the ball into play.'

Albert went back a few paces and ran forward, kicking the ball so well that everybody gasped with amazement, except Albert, who was flat on his back and could not see where the ball had gone.

With a wild, Highland whoop, Angus was off after the ball, but the manager, who had introduced himself as Mr Calder, grabbed him and pointed out that now they must get out of the way of the players. Angus was disappointed, but he helped heave the still dazed Albert to his feet and they ran to the side of the pitch.

'Now,' said Mr Calder, 'it's only right that you should both come and sit in the directors' box.'

This time it was Angus who was flabbergasted, but he soon recovered, and the two bears followed Mr Calder up the steps and into the comfortable chairs of the big open box.

Two minutes later, all three of them were yelling their heads off and Albert was madly waving his rattle encouraging their own teams to score.

At half-time there had been no score and everyone enjoyed the drinks that were passed round to ease throats hoarse with shouting.

Suddenly the manager prodded Angus and Albert and said, 'Here he is, at last.'

'Who?'

'The Duke.'

'Here!'

'Of course. Come and be introduced.'

Clutching checked cap and tam o'shanter, they were introduced to the Duke who actually *thanked* them for helping him.

'Not at all, we were very pleased to do it,' Albert managed to gasp out.

Although he was shouting and waving his rattle for the English team, Albert was secretly rather pleased when the Scottish team won by two goals to one. After saying a very contented goodbye and thank-you all round, the two bears went home by the tube train again, but Angus was too full of the match to want to do any extra riding on the moving stair.

Albert stirred up the fire and put on some coal and then he prepared a big tea, for they were very hungry. It was while they were buttering their second oatcake and Albert was passing the last pot of Extra Rich honey that Angus said, 'Why don't you come up

to Stirling next week for the Highland Games?'

'Could I?'

'Yes, of course. You'd like it very much. Caber tossing and putting the shot and wrestling and all the Scottish dancing. Will you come?'

'I certainly will. It is quite a while since I had a holiday, and I haven't seen Aunt Bertha for such a long time.'

They talked of the things they would do together in Scotland and then it was time to leave for the station. King's Cross was packed with happy, shouting Scots going home after winning the match. Angus found a seat and Albert stayed with him until the long train pulled out of the great station and he waved till it was out of sight.

As he went contentedly home, Albert thought about his coming visit to Stirling. 'I might buy myself a kilt,' he said.

●

You can also read more about Albert in *Albert on the Farm* and *Albert's Christmas*.

GEORGE SPEAKS

DICK KING-SMITH

Illustrated by Judy Brown

Imagine standing admiring your four-week-old baby brother, when he suddenly opens his eyes and calls you a pig! That's what happens to seven-year-old Laura in this marvellous book. George seems to know every word in the dictionary, and to be rather a bullying sort of baby. At first he tries to keep his talents quiet, but when he gets fed up with milk (and wet nappies), he and Laura work out a way to get him the sort of treatment he wants, and then, very gradually, they train his mother not to be too surprised. Of course, Laura has a wonderful time, especially when he helps her learn her three-times table, and his first birthday party makes a fine ending to this very funny book. After this, I'm sure you'll never look at a new baby without remembering George, and hoping there's another like him.

●

*L*aura's baby brother George was four weeks old when it happened.

Laura, who was seven, had very much wanted a brother or sister for a long time. It would be so nice to have someone to play with, she thought. But when

George was born, she wasn't so sure.

Everybody — her mother and father, the grand-parents, uncles, aunts, friends — made such a fuss of him. And all of them said how beautiful he was. Laura didn't think he was. How could anyone with a round red face and a squashy nose and little tiny eyes all sunken in fat be called beautiful? She looked at him as he lay asleep in his carry-cot.

'Don't wake George up, will you?' her mother had said. 'I'll be in the kitchen if you want me.'

'I won't wake you,' Laura said to the sleeping baby. 'And I don't want to sound rude. But I must tell you something. You look just like a little pig.'

And that was when it happened.

The baby opened his eyes and stared straight at her.

'Pig yourself,' he said.

Laura gasped. A shiver ran up her spine and her toes tingled.

'What did you say?' she whispered.

'I said, "Pig yourself",' said George. 'You're not deaf, are you?'

'No,' said Laura. 'No, it's just that I didn't expect you to say anything.'

'Why not?'

'Well, babies don't say proper words. They only make noises, like Goo-goo or Blur-blur or Wah.'

'Is that a fact?' said the baby.

'Yes,' said Laura. 'It is. However can you talk like that when you're only four weeks old? It's amazing! I must run and tell Mum.'

She turned to dash out of the room.

'Laura!' said the baby sharply.

Laura turned back.

'Yes, George?' she said.

The baby looked at her very severely, his forehead creased into a little frown.

'On no account are you to tell our mother,' he said. 'Or anyone else for that matter. This is a secret between you and me. Do you understand?'

'Yes, George,' said Laura.

'I've been waiting for some time now,' said George, 'to speak to you on your own. This is the first proper chance I've had, what with feeding and bathing and nappy-changing and people coming to see me all the time. And talk about making noises — that's all some of them do. They bend over me with silly grins on their faces, and then they come out with a load of rubbish. "Who's booful den?" "Who's a gorgeous Georgeous Porgeous?" "Diddums wassums Granny's ickle treasure?" It's an insult to the English language.'

'But George,' said Laura, 'how do you know the English language?'

'Well, I'm English, aren't I?'

'Yes, but how did you learn it?'

'Same way as you, I imagine. Listening to grown-ups talking. I wasn't born yesterday, you know.'

'But you're only four weeks old,' said Laura. 'How did you learn so quickly?'

'I'm a quick learner,' said George.

He waved his little arms and kicked his pudgy legs in the air.

'Talking's a piece of cake,' he said. 'Trouble is, I haven't learned to control my body very well yet. In fact, I'm afraid we'll have to postpone the rest of this conversation until another time.'

'Why?' asked Laura.

'I'm wet,' said George.

'Oh,' said Laura. 'Shall I go and tell Mummy you

need changing?'

'Use your brains, Laura,' said George. 'You couldn't have known unless I'd told you, could you? You keep quiet. I'll tell her.'

'But you said it was going to be a secret between the two of us — you being able to talk, I mean.'

'So it is,' said George. 'I'll tell her in the way she expects. I've got her quite well trained,' and he shut his eyes and yelled 'Wah! Wah! Wah!' at the top of his voice.

His mother came in.

'What de matter with Mummy's lubbly lickle lambie?' she said.

She picked George up and felt him.

'Oh, he's soaking!' she said. 'No wonder he was crying, poor pettikins!'

She smiled at Laura as she changed the baby's nappy. 'It's the only way they can let you know there's something wrong, isn't it?' she said.

'Yes, Mummy,' said Laura.

She caught George's eye as he lay across his mother's lap. It was no surprise to her that he winked.

NO MORE SCHOOL

WILLIAM MAYNE

Illustrated by Peter Warner

My favourite people in this book are Ruth and Shirley. They are the ones who decide to run the village school all by themselves, in spite of having no teacher and no school meals. So they do all the teaching and cooking, but they also have a few troubles, such as when the School Inspector calls (he turns out to be the electricity man), and a flood, and having to keep Fletcher and Bobby and the other twelve pupils in order when they get tired of arithmetic. This is a really interesting story – as you read it you'll be wondering if you could do as well as Ruth, who manages to get sixteen school meals out of less than £1, and you'll find yourselves as disappointed as I was when Miss Oldroyd comes back and school becomes 'ordinary' again.

●

'You've taught three times this week,' said Shirley.
'I will have, by the end of the day,' said Ruth. 'And you will next week.'

'And it was sports all yesterday morning,' said Shirley. 'So I didn't have a proper go. And now, you see, I'm getting a bit bored of it, even when I haven't managed to do any.'

'It doesn't matter what you feel today,' said Ruth. 'I'm teacher.'

Shirley was a little offended, because Ruth did not give her enough sympathy, or even offer her an extra turn. When Fletcher and Bobby began to be rebellious before they got into school Shirley watched, instead of doing something useful like pulling Fletcher's hair. Ruth had to threaten them with being sent to Burton school, as well as with the list to show Miss Oldroyd, before they would come into the school building. Then she had to pinch the backs of their necks to make them sit down. They sat down and rubbed their necks. Shirley went into the kitchen.

'Register,' said Ruth. 'That'll show if you're here, Fletcher, and if you aren't we'll get the kidcatcher and you'll get put in the dogs' home,' and she looked fiercely at Fletcher.

Shirley spoiled Ruth's bad temper by giggling behind the kitchen door.

'Well,' said Ruth, 'somebody has to catch the dogs. Now we'll have prayers.'

At playtime Fletcher pointed out that he and Bobby had behaved themselves as well as possible, ever since they had sat down in school.

'Only because I half-killed you,' said Ruth. 'I sprained my thumb when I was pinching your neck.'

'But we were good,' said Fletcher.

'Gey good,' said Bobby, 'You promised we could practise sports.'

'After playtime,' said Ruth. 'But everybody's got to keep as good as they were, because we've sent off the postcard.'

'We'll get worse if we don't practise,' said Fletcher.

'Get the things out,' said Ruth. 'I'll help Shirley.'

Shirley was sitting on the kitchen table dipping a stick of rhubarb into the sugar and sucking it, and not really thinking of the job at all. She was looking out of the window at the sky. She blinked at Ruth. 'Have a suck,' she said.

'They're playing rotten old sports,' said Ruth. 'So I'll help you.'

'Good,' said Shirley. 'Why can't you get potatoes already cooked, or with zips on or something like bananas? My thumb gets all wrinkled and chopped at the end.'

'We can always sticking-plaster it,' said Ruth. 'We haven't had to sticking-plaster anyone yet.'

'We have now,' said Shirley. Ruth picked up Shirley's hand, which was in the water with the potatoes.

'Stop it,' said Shirley, 'all the water's running down my elbow. It isn't me that's cut, but Betty. She just jumped higher than she could over the bar, and she's cut her knee.'

'Quick,' said Ruth. 'Make a hospital. Put up one of the tables.'

Bobby brought Betty in, and she stood by the door holding her knee whilst Bobby helped to put the table up. Then they made her lie on it whilst they looked at her knee.

'Which one was it?' said Ruth.

'This one,' said Betty, pointing. 'It doesn't hurt any more, though.'

'We'll wash it,' said Ruth. 'I'll get your towel, and wash it with that.'

Shirley brought a bowl of water, and they bathed the knee. It was not an easy job to do tidily. In a little while Betty began to wriggle, because the water was running along the table and getting underneath her. 'I'm lying in it,' she said.

'We're just getting down to your skin,' said Ruth.

'I know,' said Betty.

'Here we are,' said Ruth, using the dry end of the towel to wipe away the last muddy water. 'Here's the wound. Can you see it, Shirley?'

'Just to say,' said Shirley. 'It isn't very big.' She went into the schoolroom and brought back a ruler. 'It's nearly half an inch long,' she said.

'How deep?' said Betty.

'It's about as deep as the groove on a gramophone record,' said Shirley. 'We'll disinfect it, and then sticking-plaster it.'

When they had dabbed and patched the wound Betty went out to jump again. Ruth swabbed up the water on the table and said, 'We never get anything real happening, do we?'

They went back to the last few potatoes.

After dinner there was more playtime. At the end of it Bobby and Fletcher and Peter were missing.

'They went off in the fields,' said Betty. 'They said they'd finished with school.'

'Did they?' said Ruth. 'Well, we'll do something nice whilst they aren't here, and that'll teach them. The little ones can have the playhouse out in the yard, and we'll all go in the field and I'll read to you, and you can draw at the same time, and I'll give you lots of marks for the drawings, and they won't get any. And you can have a sweet to suck, because there's just enough of them without the boys. That'll cap them.'

It was really a good way to spend the afternoon, because Friday is not a hard-working day. In fact, it was really a sleepy sort of day, and Ruth found herself yawning as she read, and her eyes clouding with the big tears that yawning brings, so that she had to keep shaking her head. Then she found her elbows aching and her breath getting short, because she was lying on her front with the book on the ground. The other side of the wall the little ones were running in and out of their playhouse at the tops of their voices, and across in the fields the hay was being led in. Ruth was just going to ask one of her pupils to get her the cushion from inside so that she could curl up and relax, when she heard hard shoes running in the yard.

'Ruth,' said Fletcher's voice. 'He's coming. Where

are you at? He's just up the road.'

Fletcher looked over the wall. Ruth propped herself up to look at him. She felt like a seal reared up on its flippers.

'The inspector,' said Fletcher. 'We saw him again. He's coming. He didn't see us.'

'Lucky for you,' said Ruth. Then she realized that if the school was going to be inspected it would have to be perfect, with Susan and Bill reading hard words, and Fletcher doing his fractions perfectly. 'Quick,' she said. 'Everybody inside. Everybody be tidy.'

'Cup of tea,' said Shirley. 'That's what you give people. I'll put on the kettle. I'll fill it with hot water, and it'll be quicker.'

The top class and the middle class climbed the wall into the yard. They took the playhouse down round the little family inside it, and took it in, and shooed the little ones in after it and put them in their desks.

Ruth gave them copying of letters to do.

'Arithmetic,' she said. 'Be doing your last lot again. Fletcher, you just copy a good one from Shirley's book, and pretend you've done it. Bobby, do up your shoe. Peter, stop panting like a dog.'

Ruth pulled the arithmetic-with-answers out of the cupboard and began to do a hard-looking fraction on the board.

There was the noise of a car engine outside. It stopped.

'I'll be explaining this sum,' said Ruth. 'Now, this is three-quarters divided by one-sixth, you see, three over four divided by one over six. Can anyone tell me the special secret about dividing fractions?'

The school door rattled. Someone was trying it. The latch moved. The door began to open. The inspector stood in the doorway. He was wearing his flat-topped blue cap. He had in his hand a book. It would be his complaints book, Ruth thought.

'Here's the tea,' said Shirley, coming through with the teapot. 'Oh, he's here.'

THE WORST WITCH

JILL MURPHY

Illustrated by the Author

Mildred Hubble wasn't really a witch, she was only *learning* to be one (at Miss Cackle's Academy for Witches) and not making a very good job of it. For instance, on her second day she crashed and broke her broomstick, then she got the Laughter Spell mixed up with an Invisible one, and another time she turned Miss Hardbroom's favourite pupil into a pig. But the worst thing happened at the Flying Display because there was a bad spell on her broomstick and she messed up the last formation for everybody. In the end Mildred decided to run away and, surprisingly, that turned her into the school heroine.

The author, Jill Murphy, is also an artist, and her funny drawings make all her *Worst Witch* books extra special.

●

After the ceremony everyone rushed to see Mildred's kitten.

'I think H.B. had a hand in this somewhere,' said Maud darkly. ('H.B.' was their nickname for Miss Hardbroom.)

'I must admit, it does look a bit dim, doesn't it?' said Mildred, scratching the tabby kitten's head. 'But I don't really mind. I'll just have to think of another name — I was going to call it Sooty. Let's take them down to the playground and see what they make of broomstick riding.'

Almost all the first-year witches were in the yard trying to persuade their puzzled kittens to sit on their broomsticks. Several were already clinging on by their claws, and one kitten, belonging to a rather smug young witch named Ethel, was sitting bolt upright cleaning its paws, as if it had been broomstick riding all its life!

Riding a broomstick was no easy matter, as I have mentioned before. First, you ordered the stick to hover, and it hovered lengthways above the ground. Then you sat on it, gave it a sharp tap, and away you flew. Once in the air you could make the stick do almost anything by saying, 'Right! Left! Stop! Down a bit!' and so on. The difficult part was balancing, for if you leaned a little too far to one side you could easily overbalance, in which case you would either fall off or find yourself hanging upside-down and then you would just have to hold on with your skirt over your head until a friend came to your rescue.

It had taken Mildred several weeks of falling off and crashing before she could ride the broomstick reasonably well, and it looked as though her kitten was going to have the same trouble. When she put it on the end of the stick, it just fell off without even trying to hold on. After many attempts, Mildred picked up her kitten and gave it a shake.

'Listen!' she said severely. 'I think I shall have to call you Stupid. You don't even *try* to hold on. Everyone else is all right – look at all your friends.'

The kitten gazed at her sadly and licked her nose with its rough tongue.

'Oh, come on,' said Mildred, softening her voice. 'I'm not really angry with you. Let's try again.'

And she put the kitten back on the broomstick, from which it fell with a thud.

Maud was having better luck. Her kitten was hanging on grimly upside down.

'Oh, well,' laughed Maud. 'It's a start.'

'Mine's useless,' said Mildred, sitting on the broomstick for a rest.

'Never mind,' Maud said. 'Think how hard it must be for them to hang on by their claws.'

An idea flashed into Mildred's head, and she dived into the school, leaving her kitten chasing a leaf along the ground and the broomstick still patiently hovering. She came out carrying her satchel which she hooked over the end of the broom and then bundled the

kitten into it. The kitten's astounded face peeped out of the bag as Mildred flew delightedly round the yard.

'Look, Maud!' she called from ten feet up in the air.

'That's cheating!' said Maud, looking at the satchel.

Mildred flew back and landed on the ground laughing.

'I don't think H.B. will approve,' said Maud doubtfully.

'Quite right, Maud,' an icy voice behind them said. 'Mildred, my dear, possibly it would be even easier with handlebars and a saddle.'

Mildred blushed.

'I'm sorry, Miss Hardbroom,' she muttered. 'It doesn't balance very well – my kitten, so . . . I thought . . . perhaps . . .' Her voice trailed away under Miss Hardbroom's stony glare and Mildred unhooked her satchel and turned the bewildered kitten on to the ground.

'Girls!' Miss Hardbroom clapped her hands. 'I would remind you that there is a potion test tomorrow morning. That is all.'

So saying, she disappeared – literally.

'I wish she wouldn't do that,' whispered Maud, looking at the place where their form-mistress had been standing. 'You're never quite sure whether she's gone or not.'

'Right again, Maud,' came Miss Hardbroom's voice from nowhere.

Maud gulped and hurried back to her kitten.

●

Other stories about Mildred are to be found in *The Worst Witch Strikes Again* and *A Bad Spell for the Worst Witch*.

THE BATTLE OF BUBBLE AND SQUEAK

PHILIPPA PEARCE

Illustrated by Alan Baker

There are three friends to make in this story, because although it is Sid who brings the two gerbils (called Bubble and Squeak after his favourite food) into his home, his sisters Peggy and Amy love them just as much, and try to make their mother like them too. But Mrs Sparrow thinks they are just like dirty little rats and tries very hard to get rid of them; first by sending them back to the pet shop, then by giving them away to two boys (but *their* mother brings them back), and then she gives them to the dustmen, who also bring them back. After that she has to promise to let them stay — but there are still problems, for instance the time when Squeak escapes:

●

The gerbils came home from the Mudds' house in the last week before the Christmas holidays.

They were received with rejoicing by the children. Bill Sparrow looked on, smiling. Their mother held aloof, but there seemed no doubt that she did not feel as badly about gerbils as she had once done. She put up with them. She did not love them — any more than she loved other things she had to put up with. She put up with the draught through the back door, and old Mrs Pring's cats, and Bill Sparrow's gardening boots. She loved none of these things, but she put up with them. Now she had begun putting up with gerbils.

On the first morning after the gerbils' return, Peter Peters called early on the way to school. He wanted to see Bubble and Squeak again. Peggy left her breakfast, in the middle, to show them to him. Amy had finished her breakfast and went with her. Then Peggy came back to the kitchen, leaving Amy and Peter Peters gazing into the gerbil cage.

'Did you tell them not to take them out?' Sid asked. Peggy called to Amy from the kitchen with Sid's message.

Peggy and Sid went on with their breakfasts. Bill had nearly finished his. Mrs Sparrow was busy about the kitchen.

Amy and Peter Peters were still with the gerbils.

Dawn Mudd called. That meant it was time to set off for school.

'Come on, Amy!' her mother called. 'Or you'll be late!'

What happened next is not certain, because neither Amy nor Peter Peters were reliable witnesses. What is certain is that, disobeying Sid, Amy had taken either Bubble or Squeak out to show Peter Peters. They were stroking the gerbil when Mrs Sparrow called from the kitchen. Amy was instantly in a hurry not to be late. The gerbil was put back into the cage at once. Then, at once, Amy shut the door of the cage, and slammed the bolt across it. The bolt was made of wire, and rather light: it had to be shot home rather carefully, and Amy was in too much of a hurry to be careful. Either she did not shoot the bolt far enough, or she shot it so hard that it bounced back. Whichever happened, the door of the cage came ajar.

The enterprising gerbils took advantage of this.

The one lucky thing, as Bill Sparrow later pointed out, was that they must have escaped almost at once. They began exploring. Already Peggy and Amy, with Dawn Mudd and Peter Peters, had left for school; but the others were still in the kitchen. The door from the hall into the kitchen was open, like the door from the living-room into the hall. Mrs Sparrow, facing in that direction, gave a moan. Bill was half-way through his last cup of tea; Sid was tying his shoe-laces. Both looked up, and turned towards the point at which

Mrs Sparrow was staring.

On the threshold of the doorway sat Bubble – or was it Squeak? He sat up on his haunches, his forepaws against his chest, gazing at them all in amazement.

Sid pushed his chair back with a cry, and Bill Sparrow gave a sudden guffaw.

Squeak – or was it Bubble? – dropped suddenly on all fours, and whisked round the corner and back in the direction from which he must have come.

Sid rushed after him.

There was no sign of a gerbil in the hall by the time Sid got there, nor on the living-room floor. However, a gerbil was perched on the cushion of a chair within easy jumping distance of the top of the living-room table. That gerbil somehow looked as if it had just come from the table, not as if it were in the act of going back to it. But, of course, you couldn't be sure. Unless you were Peggy, you simply could not be sure which gerbil was which.

On the living-room table stood the cage, empty, of course, and with its door wide open.

One gerbil, but not two.

Sid made a quick dive towards the gerbil on the cushion. The gerbil made a quick dive into the narrow dark cavern formed by the leaning of the cushion against the back of the chair.

'Got you!' said Sid. He began exploring with one hand from one side of the cushion and with the other from the other. His hands met: no gerbil. The gerbil popped out suddenly from underneath the middle of the cushion. Sid whipped one hand out to catch him. His fingers closed on him, but roughly. The gerbil bit him. Sid yelped and let go. The gerbil darted back under the cushion.

'Want help?' asked Bill. He had followed Sid at leisure.

'Put in one hand here, and the other hand the other side,' directed Sid. 'And don't try to catch him with your whole hand. He's in a panic. He'll bite. Get his tail. But, anyway, he'll probably come out at the front again, and I'll catch him then.'

Bill Sparrow did as he was told. As before, the gerbil came out at the front of the cushion, where Sid was waiting for him. Sid pounced more skilfully this time, caught him by his tail, and popped him into the cage. He shut the door and bolted it carefully.

One gerbil – but not two.

His mother stood behind him. 'It's time to go. Have you got it?'

'Yes. One. But not both.'

'For Heaven's sake! A gerbil loose, and we're both going to be late for work, and you're going to miss your school bus!' She began frantically moving chairs and also cushions on chairs. The other two searched as well.

No second gerbil.

Mrs Sparrow glanced at the clock. 'You go, Bill. I'll follow.'

He went.

She eyed her son. 'I'm not going until I've seen you on to that bus, Sid.'

Plainly she meant what she said. So Sid decided to be plain with his mother, too. 'I'm not going to school until I've found my gerbil. If it's left to itself all day, anything might happen.'

'What?'

'If it got outside somehow, a cat.'

Mrs Sparrow said nothing.

'Or it could get under the floorboards and die of starvation there. And rot. And smell.'

Sid was watching his mother closely. Her expression was changing from its original firmness.

'Under the floorboards?'

'Yes.'

Suddenly she said: 'Promise me faithfully that, if you do find it by dinner-time, you'll go in to afternoon school. I'll give you money for the bus fare.'

He promised.

'Although what reason you'll give for not going this morning . . .'

'I could tell them the truth.'

Just as Mrs Sparrow was leaving the house, she stuck her head in again: 'I'll tell Mrs Pring. She'll look in to see you're all right. And you can help yourself from the fridge.'

When his mother had gone, Sid did a thorough turn out of the living-room. Somehow it looked tousled when he had finished with it. No gerbil.

But he supposed that the gerbil might have gone anywhere, even upstairs. So upstairs and downstairs Sid searched, wherever a door had been left ajar, or wherever there was a gap between the bottom of a shut door and the threshold (and the house was not a particularly well-built one). Soon most of the house began to have that tousled look.

But no gerbil.

He wondered if it were true that gerbils come back to their home cages in the end, anyway. He would have to rely on that, or on the gerbil's moving about enough to make a noise he could hear. He himself would have to be very quiet.

He took a comfortable chair out into the hall, where he hoped to be able to hear a sound — if it were loud enough — from anywhere in the house. Luckily the caged gerbil seemed asleep, so there was no noise from *him*. But Sid heard his own noises, as he fidgeted anxiously in his chair. The creak of the chair . . . the scrape of his shoe against the leg . . . and then his own breathing . . . and a cough he would have to let out . . .

But the house round him was so still that he jumped when the flap of the front door letterbox went up. He guessed it was old Mrs Pring. So it was dinner-time already.

Mrs Pring always thought of Sid as a little boy, because she had known him so long. She called through the letterbox: 'Don't be frightened, dear. I've brought you some hot soup, and I thought I'd bring you —' On the last word, her fingers must have slipped, for the word was lost in the clatter of the flap snapping down again.

Sid could see through the glass panels of the front door that the dumpy figure of Mrs Pring was burdened with two objects. One — the bowl of soup? — in her right hand; the other, a light orangey-brown colour, on or under her left arm. No wonder she hadn't managed to keep the letter-flap up for long.

Unsuspecting, Sid threw wide the front door.

In her right hand Mrs Pring carried a steaming bowl.

Under her left arm she carried her cat, Ginger.

Sid gaped at the cat, while Mrs Pring began at once to say that his mother had said there was a rat in the house, and that Sid was trying to catch it, and if so, Ginger was the one. The best ratter, the best mouser —

All the time, Mrs Pring was advancing into the house.

Sid came to life. 'No!' he cried, realizing that this was not the time for politeness. But he was already too late. Ginger — like most cats — did not like being carried for long. He had begun to wriggle, and Mrs Pring was not one to oppose her cat's wishes. She allowed Ginger to leap from her arms. He began walking down the hall towards the living-room. Sid tried to catch him. Ginger accelerated his pace just enough to escape from under Sid's hands and into the living-room. At that moment, the gerbil already in the cage decided to get out of bed. He rustled through the hay of his bedroom — and Ginger at once froze.

The gerbil moved into sight at the bars of his cage, and Ginger was crouching lower — lower — like a snake against the ground, still except for the tip of his tail, which flicked to and fro . . .

Although Sid knew that the gerbil was protected by its cage, he threw himself upon Ginger before the leap. This time he caught the cat and held him long enough to open the window and fling him out.

Ginger landed neatly on all four paws, but was displeased — one could see that. He sat down at once and began cleaning himself, as though he had never really meant to go gerbil-hunting. What he had always really intended was to clean himself in the fresh air.

Sid shut the window again, and had to face Mrs Pring.

Mrs Pring was even more offended than Ginger. She put the soup down carefully on the kitchen table and then scolded Sid like a very little boy. She said that all children should know about kindness to animals, and Ginger was such a kind cat that he should never have been thrown anywhere, let alone out of a window. He would have caught that horrid rat for Sid, wherever it had hidden itself in the house . . .

'Yes, Mrs Pring, yes,' murmured Sid.

In the end, Mrs Pring went, and Sid drank his soup in the kitchen, and made himself a cheese-and-pickle sandwich, and ate it as he sat in the hall. He began eating an apple, but found the crunching sound deafening. You couldn't listen for gerbil-noises through all that row.

He sat with the doors of the living-room and cloakroom open; also all the doors upstairs. He was giving himself the best chance of hearing any unusual sound in the house. He could also see most of the hall, and into the cloakroom and the living-room. He could even see the gerbil cage on the table in the living-room. He couldn't see the gerbil inside: it must be having its afternoon nap in its hay bed.

After a while, from the living-room, he heard the gentle little scrabbling-gnawing sound of a gerbil awake and active. In his mind, he set the sound to one side, and went on listening for the special sound of an escaped gerbil. He glanced into the living-room: still no sign of the gerbil in the cage.

Then he woke up to what that might mean.

He rose from his chair and went softly into the living-room and bent over the cage. The gerbil was buried in the hay of its bedroom. It stirred a little, as he looked, but certainly not enough to account for the sound he had heard.

Besides — there was the sound again, and it didn't come from the cage at all, but from the other side of the room. He stood absolutely still and listened. Yes, again; and from the far side of the room.

He went over on tiptoe; but, as soon as he moved, the noise stopped. They had looked behind the furniture here, and found nothing; but perhaps . . .

Suddenly, the noise again. He found that his gaze had fixed itself upon the edge of the carpet, where it met the wall. Only it wasn't exactly an edge there. Years ago Mrs Sparrow had bought the carpet second-hand. It was rather too long for the living-room, but she had not liked to cut it to size. So one end of it had been folded under. The fold of the carpet where it reached the wall made the longest, darkest, most tempting tunnel that either Bubble or Squeak could have wished for, outside Mongolia.

Sid knew in his bones that the escaped gerbil was in the carpet-tunnel.

His impulse was to rush forward, flap the carpet back, and catch the gerbil. Catch the gerbil? He found that he was trembling: he was terribly afraid that he would somehow mess it all up, and the gerbil would escape again, and get more and more panicky, and he would get more and more excited, and he would never catch his gerbil . . .

He decided what to do. He got two of the largest pieces of coal from the scuttle, and weighed down either end of the carpet tunnel. He checked that the two exits were really closed. Of course, any gerbil worth his salt could gnaw his way through a wall of carpet, but that would take a little time. Meanwhile, Sid dashed upstairs to the bathroom and brought down the empty laundry box. It was really just a deep box, standing on four legs, with a hinged lid. At each side, near the top, was a hand-hole, so that one could carry the box easily. These hand-holes would ventilate the box, when the lid was down. Here was a very simple gerbil container. He felt sure that, if only he could catch the gerbil, he could drop it into this box. If he tried to get it through the narrow cage door straight into the cage — well, he didn't trust himself. The other gerbil might be trying to get out, or he might drop this one. Or anything might happen.

It was extraordinary how nervous he felt.

He padded the bottom of the laundry box with a scarlet cushion, and left the lid up. He drew the box as near to the carpet-fold as possible. He removed the lump of coal from one end of the tunnel.

He was ready.

But there was no sound at all now from inside the tunnel. He realized that there had been no sound since he had come back from the bathroom with the box. Perhaps the gerbil had already escaped from the carpet-fold. He was almost sure that must be so. Yes, he was convinced of it. On an impulse of despair, he seized the corner of the carpet and flapped back the fold.

There was the gerbil.

Forgetting all about the wisdom of picking up a gerbil by its tail, he clapped his hands over it quickly, roughly. The gerbil bit him, but he hardly noticed.

Down into the laundry box, and slam the lid!

He had his gerbil. He had them both – Bubble and Squeak.

He laughed aloud. The thought of school never occurred to him — and indeed it was much too late for that, anyway. He began to dance, like a teetotum. Faster and faster, round and round, laughing. He stopped only when he found himself staggering about the room, giddy. He stopped, and fell crazily on the couch. His head was rocking. He lay with closed eyes. His mind became delightfully muddled.

He slept.

When the others came home, they found him asleep on the couch, and the gerbil — it was Squeak, Peggy said — safe in the laundry box. It had gnawn a hole in the scarlet cushion cover and down into the stuffing of the cushion. That was all.

Everyone was pleased at the happy end of the story. Sid hardly scolded Amy. Even Mrs Sparrow, looking at the gnawn cushion cover, only said: 'Well, you can't have too many dusters.'

But that wasn't really the end of the story.

By now it was quite dark outside, so that no one in the house noticed someone outside, peering in: Ginger. The house held a fascination for him.

●

Philippa Pearce has written another book which I'm sure you will enjoy. It's called *Lion at School and Other Stories*.

MRS PEPPERPOT IN THE MAGIC WOOD

ALF PRØYSEN

Illustrated by Björn Berg

Imagine how you'd feel if, without any warning, you suddenly became so small that you could be picked up by a bird, or trodden on by a big boot, or dropped into a teacup? Well, all those things, and worse, happened to Mrs Pepperpot, though sometimes they could be exciting as well. There was the time she sat on her husband's shoulder and went skiing, or when she met the little people who lived in the magic wood and was carried away by some crows. In fact, whatever happened to Mrs Pepperpot when she shrank, she never got really frightened, and things usually turned out all right. Here she is being taught to swim, by a frog:

●

As you know, Mrs Pepperpot can do almost any-thing, but for a long time there was one thing she couldn't do; she couldn't swim! Now I'll tell you how she learned.

In the warm weather Mrs Pepperpot always took a short cut through the wood when she went shopping. In the middle of the wood is quite a large pool which

the village children use. Here they play and splash about in the water. The older ones, who can swim, dive from a rock and race each other up and down the pool. They teach the younger ones to swim too, as there's no grown-up to show them. Luckily, the pool is only deep round the big rock and those who can't swim stay where it's shallow. But they're all very keen to learn, so they practise swimming-strokes lying on their tummies over a tree-stump and counting one-two-three-four as they stretch and bend their arms and legs.

Mrs Pepperpot always stopped to watch them, and then she would sigh to herself and think: 'If only I could do that!' Because nobody had taught *her* to swim when she was a little girl.

Some of the big boys could do the crawl, and the little ones tried to copy them, churning up the water with their feet and their arms going like windmills while everyone choked and spluttered.

'I bet I could learn that too!' thought Mrs Pepperpot. 'But where could I practise?'

One day when she got home, she decided to try some swimming-strokes in the kitchen, but no sooner had she got herself balanced on her tummy over the kitchen stool, when her neighbour knocked on the door asking to borrow a cup of flour. Another time she tried, she flung out her arms and knocked the saucepan of soup off the stove, and her husband had to have bread and dripping for supper. He was *not* pleased.

Every night she would dream about swimming. One night she had a lovely dream in which she could do the breast-stroke most beautifully. As she dreamed, she stretched forward her arms, bent her knees and then – Wham! One foot almost kicked a hole in the wall, the other knocked Mr Pepperpot out of bed!

Mr Pepperpot sat up. 'What's the matter with you?' he muttered. 'Having a nightmare, or something?'

'Oh no,' answered Mrs Pepperpot, who was still half in a dream. 'I'm swimming, and it's the most wonderful feeling!'

'Well, it's not wonderful for me, I can tell you!' said Mr Pepperpot crossly. 'You stop dreaming and let me have some peace and quiet.' And he climbed into bed and went to sleep again.

But Mrs Pepperpot couldn't stop dreaming about swimming. Another night she dreamed she was doing the crawl — not like the little ones, all splash and noise, but beautiful, strong, steady strokes like the big boys, and one arm went up and swept the flower-pots from the window-sill and the other landed smack on Mr Pepperpot's nose.

This was too much for Mr Pepperpot. He sat up in bed and shook Mrs Pepperpot awake.

'You stop that, d'you hear!' he shouted.

'I was only doing the crawl,' said Mrs Pepperpot in a far-away voice.

'I don't care if you were doing a high dive or a somersault!' Mr Pepperpot was very angry now. 'All I know is you need water for swimming and not a bed. If you want to swim go jump in a swimming pool and get yourself a swimming teacher!'

'That's too expensive,' said Mrs Pepperpot, who was now awake. 'I watch the children in the pool in the wood. One of these days, when they're all gone home, I'll have a try myself.'

'Catch your death of cold, no doubt,' muttered Mr Pepperpot and dozed off again. But a little while later there was a terrible crash, and this time Mr Pepperpot nearly jumped out of his skin.

There was Mrs Pepperpot, on the floor, rubbing a large lump on her forehead. She had been trying to dive off the side of the bed!

'You're the silliest woman I ever knew!' said Mr

Pepperpot. 'And I've had enough! I'm going to sleep on the kitchen floor.'

With that he gathered up the eiderdown and a pillow, went into the kitchen and slammed the door.

Mrs Pepperpot was a bit puzzled. 'I can't have done it right!' But then she decided enough was enough and, wrapping herself in the only blanket that was left on the bed, she slept the rest of the night without any more swimming-dreams.

Then came a bright warm day when all the village children were going on a picnic up in the mountains.

'That's good,' thought Mrs Pepperpot, 'there'll be no one in the pool today and I can get my chance to have a try.'

So when she'd cleaned the house and fed the cat and the dog, she walked through the wood to the pool.

It certainly looked inviting, with the sun shining

down through the leaves and making pretty patterns on the still water. There was no one else about.

She sat down on the soft grass and took off her shoes and stockings. She had brought a towel with her, but she'd never owned a bathing suit, and it didn't even occur to her to take her skirt and blouse off. Peering over the edge, she could see the water wasn't very deep just there, so she stood up and said to herself: 'All right, Mrs P., here goes!' and she jumped in!

But she might have known it – at this moment she SHRANK!

Down, down she went, and now, of course, the pool seemed like an ocean to the tiny Mrs Pepperpot.

'Help, help!' she cried, 'I'm drowning!'

'Hold on!' said a deep throaty voice from below. 'Rescue on the way!' And a large frog swam smoothly towards her.

'Get on my back,' he said.

Mrs Pepperpot was thrashing about with both arms and legs and getting tangled up in her skirt as well, but she managed to scramble on to the frog's knobbly back.

'Thanks!' she panted, as they came to the top, and she spat out a lot of water.

The frog swam quickly to the rock, which now seemed quite a mountain to Mrs Pepperpot, but she found a foothold all right and sat down to get her breath, while the frog hopped up beside her.

'You're certainly a good swimmer,' said Mrs Pepperpot.

The frog puffed himself up importantly: 'I'm the champion swimming teacher in this pool,' he said.

'D'you think you could teach me to swim?' asked Mrs Pepperpot.

'Of course. We'll begin right away, if you like.'

'The children do the breast-stroke first, I've noticed,' said Mrs Pepperpot.

'That's right, and frogs are very good at that. You climb on my back and watch what I do,' said the frog, as he jumped in.

It was a bit difficult to get off the rock on to the frog's back, but he trod water skilfully and kept as steady as he could. Soon she was safely perched and watched how the frog moved his arms and legs in rhythm. After a while he found her a little piece of floating wood and told her to hang on to that while she pushed herself along with her legs.

She got on fine with this till suddenly she lost her grip on the piece of wood and found herself swimming along on her own.

'Yippee!' she shouted with excitement, but the frog, who had been swimming close to her all the time, now came up below her and lifted her on to his back.

'That's enough for the moment,' he said, and took her back to the rock for a rest.

●

You can join Mrs Pepperpot on some more adventures in *Mrs Pepperpot to the Rescue.*

ABOUT TEDDY ROBINSON

JOAN G. ROBINSON

Illustrated by the Author

Practically everyone has one unchanging friend who lasts through all their growing up, and it's usually a teddy bear. Teddy Robinson was Deborah's favourite bear, and Deborah was Teddy Robinson's favourite little girl, so everything they did together was fun. For instance, when Teddy Robinson had a roundabout ride, or went to a party and won the Musical Bumps, or was drawn to be put in a book, and even when Deborah had to go into hospital and Teddy went along to cheer her up. But of course there were a few less happy adventures, like the time Deborah left him in the garden all night:

●

Then Teddy Robinson noticed that the sun was going down and there were long shadows in the garden. It looked as if it must be getting near bed-time.

Deborah will come and fetch me soon, he thought; and he watched the birds flying home to their nests in the trees above him.

A blackbird flew quite close to him and whistled and chirped, 'Good night, teddy bear.'

'Good night, bird,' said Teddy Robinson and waved an arm at him.

Then a snail came crawling past.

'Are you sleeping out tonight? That will be nice for you,' he said. 'Good night, teddy bear.'

'Good night, snail,' said Teddy Robinson, and he watched it crawl slowly away into the long grass.

She will come and fetch me soon, he thought. It must be getting quite late.

But Deborah didn't come and fetch him. Do you know why? She was fast asleep in bed!

This is what had happened. When she had run to see who was knocking at the front door, Deborah had found Uncle Michael standing on the doorstep. He had come in his new car, and he said there was just time to take her out for a ride if she came quickly, but she must hurry because he had to get into the town before tea-time. There was only just time for Mummy to get Deborah's coat on and wave goodbye before they were off. They had come home ever so much later than they meant to because they had tea out in a shop, and then on the way home the new car had suddenly stopped and it took Uncle Michael a long time to find out what was wrong with it.

By the time they reached home Deborah was half asleep, and Mummy had bundled her into bed before she had time to really wake up again and remember about Teddy Robinson still being in the garden.

He didn't know all this, of course, but he guessed

something unusual must have happened to make Deborah forget about him.

Soon a little wind blew across the garden, and down fluttered some blossom from the almond-tree. It fell right in the middle of Teddy Robinson's tummy.

'Thank you,' he said, 'I like pink flowers for a blanket.'

So the almond-tree shook its branches again, and more and more blossoms came tumbling down.

The garden tortoise came tramping slowly past.

'Hallo, teddy bear,' he said. 'Are you sleeping out? I hope you won't be cold. I felt a little breeze blowing up just now. I'm glad I've got my house with me.'

'But I have a fur coat,' said Teddy Robinson, 'and pink blossom for a blanket.'

'So you have,' said the tortoise. 'That's lucky. Well, good night,' and he drew his head into his shell and went to sleep close by.

The next-door kitten came padding softly through the grass and rubbed against him gently.

'You *are* out late,' she said.

'Yes, I think I'm sleeping out tonight,' said Teddy Robinson.

'Are you?' said the kitten. 'You'll love that. I did it once, I'm going to do it a lot oftener when I'm older. Perhaps I'll stay out tonight.'

But just then a window opened in the house next door and a voice called, 'Puss! Puss! Puss! Come and have your fish! fish! fish!' and the kitten scampered off as fast as she could go.

Teddy Robinson heard the window shut down and then everything was quiet again.

The sky grew darker and darker blue, and soon the stars came out. Teddy Robinson lay and stared at them without blinking, and they twinkled and shone and winked at him as if they were surprised to see a teddy bear lying in the garden.

And after a while they began to sing to him, a very soft and sweet and far-away little song, to the tune of *Rock-a-Bye Baby*, and it went something like this:

'Rock-a-bye Teddy, go to sleep soon.
We will be watching, so will the moon.
When you awake with dew on your paws
Down will come Debbie and take you indoors.'

Teddy Robinson thought that was a lovely song,

so when it was finished he sang one back to them. He sang it in a grunty voice because he was rather shy, and it went something like this:

> 'This is me
> under the tree,
> the bravest bear you ever did see.
> All alone
> so brave I've grown,
> I'm camping out on my very own.'

The stars nodded and winked and twinkled to show that they liked Teddy Robinson's song, and then they sang *Rock-a-bye Teddy* all over again, and he stared and stared at them until he fell asleep.

●

Other stories about Teddy Robinson are *Dear Teddy Robinson*, *Keeping up with Teddy Robinson* and *Teddy Robinson Himself*.

CAPTAIN PUGWASH AND THE PIGWIG

JOHN RYAN

Illustrated by the Author

There are such a lot of books about Captain Pugwash (the bravest, most handsome and *laziest* pirate who sailed the seven seas) that it seems best just to tell you a little about him and his crew and his fearful enemy, Cut-throat Jake and, most important, his cabin boy, Tom, and leave you to read about his adventures.

Well, to start with, the crew didn't do any work at all, they just lazed around the deck playing games, while Tom did everything, like steering the ship and making the tea.

Of course, being a pirate, Captain Pugwash is always interested in finding treasure, but he is too lazy to do much about it, and really the thing he cares about most is food. And unlike a lot of pirate captains, he doesn't even have a parrot . . .

●

*I*t was the Captain's birthday, and his crew wanted to give him a present.

They thought of an eye-patch, but that reminded them of their worst enemy, Cut-throat Jake. They thought of a wooden leg, but remembered that Pug-

wash already had two perfectly good legs.

So, in the end, they decided on a parrot.

'Every pirate should have one,' said the Mate.

'Ar ... and they come cheap round here,' said Barnabas.

So, as the ship was in harbour, they went ashore and bought the least expensive parrot they could find.

'Happy Birthday, dear Cap'n,' sang all the pirates together as they gave Pugwash his present.

'Happy Birthday!' sang the parrot ... and bit the Captain on the nose.

'Ouch! ... er, yes, er, well ... thank you very much,' said Pugwash. He wasn't very fond of birds, and had already taken a strong dislike to this one.

'I take it,' he said, as he stuck a plaster on to his nose, 'that you have bought a *cage* for the creature?'

'No cage, Cap'n,' said the Mate.

'Money ran out,' said Barnabas.

'Christmas is coming,' said Willy.

'You'll have to keep it in your cabin, Cap'n,' said the Mate, and because he didn't want to hurt the crew's feelings, Captain Pugwash agreed.

So Tom the cabin boy, who seemed to get along quite well with the parrot, took it and made it comfortable in the Captain's cabin.

But sadly, right from the start, the birthday present was *not* a success.

The parrot snapped at its new owner whenever Pugwash came within reach ... and also started to imitate the Captain in a very rude manner.

It took to repeating his favourite sayings, like 'What-ho, me hearties!' or 'Shuddering sharks!' or 'Jumping jellyfish!' Sometimes it shouted out orders in the Captain's voice, like 'Splice the mainbrace!' which means 'Free rum for all!'

This made the crew, who loved their rum, very happy, and the Captain, who was as mean as anything, very cross.

But the parrot did worse than that. Every day after lunch, the Captain liked to take a little snooze. When he snoozed, he snored. And when he snored, the parrot imitated his snoring. He did it so cleverly that nobody could tell the difference. The parrot's snoring became so loud that the Captain couldn't sleep at night, let alone after lunch!

One afternoon, Pugwash got fed up with trying to

sleep. So he decided to take a walk into town with the
crew. Little did he realize that his enemy, Cut-throat
Jake, was lurking near by and planning a raid on the
Black Pig.

In fact, that very afternoon, thinking that the Captain would be asleep as usual, Jake sneaked up the
gangplank, across the deck, and along to the Captain's
cabin. The only person in sight was Tom the cabin
boy, and for once Tom seemed quite friendly.

'Looking for the Cap'n?' Tom asked. 'Listen!'

Then, with his ear to the Captain's door, Jake heard
the Captain's voice. 'Battling barnacles! It's my bed-
time!' said the voice, and there followed a lot of loud
snoring.

'Ha-harrh! . . . asleep, eh? . . . caught like a lobster in
a pot,' breathed Jake. Waving his cutlass, he rushed
into the cabin. The Captain wasn't there, of course . . .
but the parrot was! It took one look at the intruder,
and went for him!

Cut-throat Jake was a savage fighter, but he was no match for the parrot! Pecked and scratched and bitten, he fled in terror out of the cabin, off the ship, and away down the quayside. And that was what Captain Pugwash and his crew saw as they strolled back to the *Black Pig*.

'Well, well, well,' said Pugwash, 'it's that old villain, Cut-throat Jake. We shan't see *him* again for a while, by the look of it!

'Nor,' he added to himself with a happy smile, 'my birthday parrot!'

CLEVER POLLY AND THE STUPID WOLF

CATHERINE STORR

Polly didn't know she was clever, she just didn't want to be gobbled up by the wolf, so she had to think of ways to stop him. The first time was when she was very young, and she made him burn his mouth with hot toffee. After that she hoped he'd gone away for good, but he came back, even more stupid. So when he kept saying 'I'm going to eat you up', she persuaded him to think about something else, like finding a way to climb up to her bedroom window (he tried planting a bean like Jack in *Jack and the Beanstalk*), or going to find her grandmother by underground train, or making himself invisible. Once he got caught and put in the zoo, and in the very last story he gets so stupid that she makes him start picking all the daisies in the world — so it seems as if she will grow up safely instead of being a nice plump little girl who he manages to get his teeth into.

In the meantime, here is Polly sitting happily in the garden when the wolf pays her a visit:

●

*P*olly was sitting in the garden making a daisy chain. She had grown her right thumb nail especially long on purpose to be able to do this, which meant that for the last two weeks she had said to her mother, 'Please don't cut the nail on that thumb, I need it long.' And her mother obligingly hadn't. Now it was beautifully long and only a little black. Polly slit up fat pink stalk after fat pink stalk. The daisy chain grew longer and longer.

As she worked, Polly talked to herself. It was half talking, half singing.

'Monday's child is fair of face,' she said. 'Tuesday's child is full of grace. Wednesday's child —'

'Is good to fry,' interrupted the wolf. He was looking hungrily over the garden wall.

'That's not right,' said Polly indignantly. 'It's Wednesday's child is full of woe, Thursday's child has far to go. There's nothing about frying in it at all.'

'There's nothing about woe, or going far in the poem I know,' protested the wolf. 'What would be the use of that?'

'The use?' Polly repeated. 'It isn't meant to be useful, exactly. It's just to tell you what children are like when they're born on which days.'

'Which days?' the wolf asked, puzzled.

'Well, any day, then.'

'But which is a Which Day?'

'Oh dear,' said Polly. 'Perhaps I didn't explain very well. Look, Wolf! If you're born on a Monday you'll be fair of face, because that is what the poem says. And if you're born on a Tuesday you'll be full of grace. See?'

'I'd rather be full of food,' the wolf murmured, 'I don't think grace sounds very satisfying.'

'And if you're born on a Wednesday you'll be full of woe,' said Polly, taking no notice of the interruption.

'Worse than grace,' the wolf said. 'But my poem's quite different. My poem says that Wednesday's child is good to fry. That's much more useful than knowing that it's full of woe. What good does it do anyone to know that? My poem is a useful poem.'

'Is it all about frying?' Polly asked.

The wolf thought for a moment.

'No,' he said presently. 'None of the rest of it is about frying. But it's good. It tells you the sort of things you want to know. Useful information.'

'Is it all about cooking?' Polly asked severely.

'Well, yes, most of it. But it's about children too,' the wolf said eagerly.

'That's disgusting,' said Polly.

'It isn't, it's most interesting. And instructive. For instance, I can probably guess what day of the week you were born on, Polly.'

'What day?'

The wolf looked at Polly carefully. Then he looked up at the sky and seemed to be repeating something silently to himself.

'Either a Monday or a Friday,' he said at last.

'It was a Monday,' Polly admitted. 'But you could have guessed that from my poem.'

'What does yours say?' the wolf asked.

'Monday's child is fair of face, Tuesday's child is full of grace, and I am fair, in the hair anyway,' Polly said.

'Go on. Say the whole poem.'

Polly said:

'Monday's child is fair of face,
Tuesday's child is full of grace,
Wednesday's child is full of woe,
Thursday's child has far to go.
Friday's child is loving and giving,
Saturday's child works hard for its living.
But the child that is born on the Sabbath day
Is bonny and blithe and good and gay.'

'Pooh,' cried the wolf. 'What a namby-pamby poem! There isn't a single thing I'd want to know about a child in the whole thing. And, anyway, most of it you could see with half an eye directly you met the child.'

'You couldn't see that it had far to go,' Polly argued.

'No,' the wolf agreed. 'That's the best line certainly. But it depends how far it had to go, doesn't it? I mean if it had gone a long, long way from home you might be able just to snap it up without any fuss. But then it might be tough from taking so much exercise. Not really much help.'

'It isn't meant to be much help in the way you mean,' said Polly.

'And it isn't what I call a poem, either,' the wolf added.

'Why?' asked Polly. 'It rhymes, doesn't it?'

'Oh, rhymes,' said the wolf scornfully. 'Yes, if that's all you want. It jingles along if that satisfies you. No, I meant it doesn't make you go all funny inside like real poetry does. It doesn't bring tears to your eyes and make you feel you understand life for the first time, like proper poetry.'

'Is the poem you know proper poetry?' Polly asked suspiciously.

'Certainly it is,' the wolf said indignantly. 'I'll say it to you and then you'll see.

> Monday's child is fairly tough,
> Tuesday's child is tender enough,
> Wednesday's child is good to fry,
> Thursday's child is best in pie.
> Friday's child makes good meat roll,
> Saturday's child is casserole.
> But the child that is born on the Sabbath day
> Is delicious when eaten in any way.

Now you can't hear that without having some pretty terrific feelings, can you?'

The wolf clasped his paws over his stomach and looked longingly at Polly.

'It gives me a queer tingling feeling in my inside,' he went on. 'Like a sort of beautiful, hungry pain. As if I could eat a whole lot of meals put together and not be uncomfortable afterwards. Now I'm sure your poem doesn't make you feel like that?'

'No, it doesn't,' Polly admitted.

'Does it make you feel anything?' the wolf persisted.

'No-o-o. But I like it. I shall have my children born on Sunday and then they'll be like what the poem says.'

'That would be nice,' agreed the wolf. 'But one very seldom gets a Sunday child. I believe they're delicious, even if you eat them without cooking at all!'

'I didn't mean to eat,' said Polly coldly. 'I meant children of my own. Bonny and blithe and all that.'

'What day did you say you were born on?' the wolf inquired. 'Did you say Monday or Friday?'

'Monday,' said Polly; 'fair of face.'

'Fairly tough,' said the wolf thoughtfully to himself. 'Still, there's always steaming,' he added. 'Or stewing in a very slow oven. Worth trying, I think.'

He made a bound over the garden wall on to the lawn. But Polly had been too quick for him. She had run into the house and shut the door behind her before the wolf had recovered his balance from landing on the grass.

'Ah well,' sighed the wolf, picking himself up. 'These literary discussions! Very often don't get one anywhere. A tough proposition, this Polly. I'll concentrate on something tenderer and easier to get for today.'

And picking up the daisy chain, which Polly had left behind her, he wound it round his ears and trotted peacefully out of the garden and away down the road.

•

There are two other books about Polly and the Wolf; they are *Polly and the Wolf Again*, and *Tales of Polly and the Hungry Wolf*. I really think their conversations with each other are the best I've ever read.

DANNY FOX

DAVID THOMSON

Illustrated by Gunvor Edwards

Danny Fox is, as he tells everyone, 'the handsomest and cleverest fox that ever lived', but what *I* like best about him are his children, Lick, Chew and Swallow. With names like that, I expect you can guess that they are always hungry, but they are also good and brave. They protect Doxie, their mother, when they think Daddy is dead. He never is, of course. He just gets into a few difficulties when he's trying to get food for them, such as being carried off by an eagle and dropped on an island when he can't swim, or being caught by his enemy the fisherman. In the end, though, he helps the fisherman to marry the Princess.

Here he is playing his very first trick on the poor fisherman:

●

Danny trotted along and he trotted along, feeling very hungry. The smell of fish got stronger and stronger, and the more he smelt it the hungrier he grew. His mouth watered, his pink tongue hung out and saliva dribbled from it on to the road. He sniffed and sniffed and began to run fast. Then he came round a corner and suddenly stopped.

He saw a horse and cart in front of him. The horse was walking very slowly, the driver seemed to be asleep and the cart was loaded with boxes of fish, all gleaming silver.

Danny Fox walked very quietly, one step at a time. Then he ran very quietly with his bushy tail stretched out behind him and his long smooth nose pointing up towards the cart. When he was near enough he sprang on to the cart and grabbed a fish from one of the open boxes. The driver did not look round. Danny Fox lay down very quietly, hoping not to wake him. His plan was to eat one fish, then pick up as many as he could hold in his mouth and jump off the cart and run home with them. He took a little mouthful of fish and the driver did not look round. He took a bigger mouthful of fish and the driver did not look round. Danny Fox watched him for a moment and saw that his hair was black and curly. He looked young and slim and strong.

'What a pity,' thought Danny, 'I wish he was old and slow!' And he lay down very quietly, hoping not to wake him. And crunch, crunch, crunch, he took a great big noisy mouthful and the driver jumped up and brought his whip down — swish! — on the white tip of his tail. Danny Fox leapt off the cart and over a stone wall into a field.

Now he was very unhappy. He had eaten three mouthfuls of fish, but had nothing to bring home to

Lick, Chew and Swallow, and nothing for Doxie either. The cart had gone on but — 'sniff, sniff, sniff' — he could still smell the fish as he lay hiding behind the wall.

He lay and he lay and he thought and he thought, till he thought of a plan. Then he got up quickly and he ran and he ran, keeping close behind the wall so that the driver of the cart could not see him. He ran till he came to a place where the road turned a corner, and by now the cart was far behind him. Then he jumped over the wall and lay down in the middle of the road pretending to be dead.

He lay there a long time. He heard the cart coming nearer and nearer. He kept his eyes shut. He hoped the driver would see him and not run him over.

When the driver saw Danny lying stretched in the middle of the road, he stopped his cart and said, 'That's funny. That's the fox that was stealing my fish. That's the fox I hit with my whip. I thought I had only touched the tip of his tail, but now I see I must have hurt him badly. He must have run away from me ahead of my cart. And now he is dead.' He got down from his cart and stooped to look at Danny.

'What a beautiful red coat he's got,' the driver said, 'and what beautiful, thick red trousers. What a beautiful long bushy tail, with a beautiful white tip. What a beautiful long smooth nose with a beautiful black tip. I'll take him home with me, I think, and skin him and sell his fur.'

So he picked up Danny Fox and threw him on to the cart on top of the boxes of fish. The cart went on. Danny opened one eye and saw the driver's back was turned to him. Then very quietly, he slid the tip of his tail underneath a fish and flicked it on to the road. He lay quite still and threw another fish out with his tail, then another and another and another, till all down the road behind the cart there was a long, long line of fish stretching into the distance. And the driver never looked round because he thought Danny was dead. At the next corner, Danny jumped off the cart and ran

back down the road. When the cart was out of sight, he started to pick the fish up.

He picked up one for Lick. He picked up one for Chew. He picked up one for Swallow. He tried to pick up one for Doxie too but his mouth was too full, so off he ran towards home with three fishes' heads sticking out from one side of his mouth and three fishes' tails sticking out from the other.

He ran past the farm, and the duck and the goose and the hen were watching him.

'Look out,' said the duck. 'There goes Danny Fox!'

'That's funny,' said the goose, 'he has grown new whiskers.'

'Those aren't whiskers,' said the hen.

'Yes, they are,' said the goose.

'No, they're not,' said the hen.

'What are they, then?' said the duck.

'They are three fishes' heads on one side of his mouth,' said the hen, 'and three fishes' tails on the other.'

Danny ran along the bottom of the mountain past the mouse's hole. The mouse was peeping out.

'That's funny,' said the mouse. 'I can see three fishes running along. But they have legs like a fox.'

'Fishes don't have legs,' said the pigeon who was flying up above.

'Yes, they do,' said the mouse.

'No, they don't,' said the pigeon.

'These ones do,' said the mouse.

Danny Fox ran up the mountain past the crack in the rocks where the rabbit was hiding.

'That's funny,' said the rabbit. 'Danny Fox has been out fishing. I didn't know he had a boat.'

At last Danny reached home. He threw one fish to Lick, and one fish to Chew and one fish to Swallow and while they were licking and chewing and swallowing he said to their mother, 'Come quickly with me.'

Doxie and Danny Fox ran down the mountain again till they came to the road — and after they had eaten three fish each, they picked up three fish each and carried them home. Then they went back for another three fish each, and another three fish each and another three fish each. They went on all morning carrying fish up the mountain, until there were no more left on the road.

So Danny and Doxie and Lick and Chew and Swallow had an enormous feast. They ate and they ate until they could eat no more. Then they all fell down together in a heap, fast asleep.

●

There are more stories about Danny to be found in *Danny Fox at the Palace* and *Danny Fox Meets a Stranger*.

THE OWL WHO WAS AFRAID
OF THE DARK

JILL TOMLINSON

Illustrated by Joanne Cole

How could you help loving a little owl whose name was
Plop, and who was fat and fluffy with big round eyes,
even if he broke all the owl rules by being afraid of the
dark? He said it was black and nasty, he did not like it AT
ALL, and he would rather be a day bird.

But Mrs Barn Owl said he was wrong, and he must go
into the world and find out for himself, so he tumbled off
his branch and did seven somersaults before he landed on
the ground. However, he wasn't frightened, once he had
had a chance to talk to quite a lot of interesting people,
like the boy scouts camping round their fire, or the old
lady who enjoyed sitting in the dark with her memories,
or the man with the telescope who showed him the stars,
or, best of all, Orion the black cat who took him hunting,
and so at last he agreed that 'dark is beautiful'. Here he is
on the first of his adventures:

●

'You *can't* be afraid of the dark,' said his mummy.
'Owls are *never* afraid of the dark.'
'This one is,' Plop said.

'But owls are *night* birds,' she said.

Plop looked down at his toes. 'I don't want to be a night bird,' he mumbled. 'I want to be a day bird.'

'You *are* what you *are*,' said Mrs Barn Owl firmly.

'Yes, I know,' agreed Plop, 'and what I are is afraid of the dark.'

'Oh dear,' said Mrs Barn Owl. It was clear that she was going to need a lot of patience. She shut her eyes and tried to think how best she could help Plop not to be afraid. Plop waited.

His mother opened her eyes again. 'Plop, you are only afraid of the dark because you don't know about it. What *do* you know about the dark?'

'It's black,' said Plop.

'Well, that's wrong for a start. It can be silver or blue or grey or lots of other colours, but almost never black. What else do you know about it?'

'I don't like it,' said Plop. 'I do not like it AT ALL.'

'That's not *knowing* something,' said his mother. 'That's *feeling* something. I don't think you know anything about the dark at all.'

'Dark is nasty,' Plop said loudly.

'You don't know that. You have never had your beak outside the nest-hole after dusk. I think you had better go down into the world and find out a lot more about the dark before you make up your mind about it.'

'Now?' said Plop.

'Now,' said his mother.

Plop climbed out of the nest-hole and wobbled along the branch outside. He peeped over the edge. The world seemed to be a very long way down.

'I'm not a very good lander,' he said. 'I might spill myself.'

'Your landing will improve with practice,' said his mother. 'Look! There's a little boy down there on the edge of the wood collecting sticks. Go and talk to him about it.'

'Now?' said Plop.

'Now,' said his mother. So Plop shut his eyes, took a deep breath, and fell off his branch.

His small white wings carried him down, but, as he said, he was not a good lander. He did seven very fast somersaults past the little boy.

'Ooh!' cried the little boy. 'A giant Catherine-wheel!'

'Actually,' said the Catherine-wheel, picking himself up, 'I'm a Barn Owl.'

'Oh yes — so you are,' said the little boy with obvious disappointment. 'Of course, you couldn't be a firework yet. Dad says we can't have the fireworks until it gets dark. Oh, I wish it would hurry up and get dark *soon*.'

'You *want* it to get dark?' said Plop in amazement.

'Oh, YES,' said the little boy. 'DARK IS EXCITING. And tonight is specially exciting because we're going to have fireworks.'

'What are fireworks?' asked Plop. 'I don't think owls have them — not Barn Owls, anyway.'

'Don't you?' said the little boy. 'Oh, you poor thing. Well, there are rockets, and flying saucers, and volcanoes, and golden rain, and sparklers, and . . .'

'But what *are* they?' begged Plop. 'Do you eat them?'

'NO!' laughed the little boy. 'Daddy sets fire to their tails and they *whoosh* into the air and fill the sky with coloured stars — well, the rockets, that is. I'm allowed to hold the sparklers.'

'What about the volcanoes? And the golden rain? What do they do?'

'Oh, they sort of burst into showers of stars. The golden rain *pours* — well, like rain.'

'And the flying saucers?'

'Oh, they're super! They whizz round your head and make a sort of *wheeee* noise. I like them best.'

'I think I would like fireworks,' said Plop.

'I'm sure you would,' the little boy said. 'Look here, where do you live?'

'Up in that tree — in the top flat. There are squirrels farther down.'

'That big tree in the middle of the field? Well, you can watch our fireworks from there! That's our garden – the one with the swing. You look out as soon as it gets dark . . .'

'Does it *have* to be dark?' asked Plop.

'Of course it does! You can't see fireworks unless it's dark. Well, I must go. These sticks are for the bonfire.'

'Bonfire?' said Plop. 'What's that?'

'You'll see if you look out tonight. Goodbye!'

'Goodbye,' said Plop, bobbing up and down in a funny little bow.

He watched the boy run across the field, and then took a little run himself, spread his wings, and fluttered up to the landing branch. He slithered along it on his tummy and dived head first into the nest-hole.

'Well?' said his mother.

'The little boy says DARK IS EXCITING.'

'And what do you think, Plop?'

'I still do not like it AT ALL,' said Plop, 'but I'm going to watch the fireworks – if you will sit by me.'

'I will sit by you,' said his mother.

'So will I,' said his father, who had just woken up. 'I

like fireworks.'

So that is what they did.

When it began to get dark, Plop waddled to the mouth of the nest-hole and peered out cautiously.

'Come on, Plop! I think they're starting,' called Mr Barn Owl. He was already in position on a big branch at the very top of the tree. 'We shall see beautifully from here.'

Plop took two brave little steps out of the nest-hole.

'I'm here,' said his mother quietly. 'Come on.'

So together, wings almost touching, they flew up to join Mr Barn Owl.

They were only just in time. There were flames leaping and crackling at the end of the little boy's garden. 'That must be the bonfire!' squeaked Plop.

Hardly had Plop got his wings tucked away, when 'WHOOSH!' – up went a rocket and spat out a shower of green stars. 'Ooooh!' said Plop, his eyes like saucers.

A fountain of dancing stars sprang up from the

ground – and another and another. 'Ooooh!' said Plop again.

'You sound like a Tawny owl,' said his father. 'Goodness! What's that?'

Something was whizzing about leaving bright trails of squiggles behind it and making a loud 'Wheeee!' noise.

'Oh, that's a flying saucer,' said Plop.

'Really?' his father said. 'I've never seen one of those before. You seem to know all about it. What's that fizzy one that keeps jigging up and down?'

'I expect that's my friend with a sparkler. Oooooh! There's a me!'

'I beg your pardon?' said Plop's father.

'It's a Catherine-wheel! The little boy thought I was a Catherine-wheel when I landed. Oh, isn't it beautiful? And he thought *I* was one!'

Mr Barn Owl watched the whirling, sparking circles spinning round and round.

'That must have been quite a landing!' he said.

GOBBOLINO THE WITCH'S CAT

URSULA MORAY WILLIAMS

Illustrated by the Author

There are quite a lot of cats in this book, as you will discover. And they are all either interesting or clever – but Gobbolino is my *absolute* favourite because he is so good and loving in spite of being a witch's cat. Well, actually he's only half a one, because he has blue eyes and a white paw, and all he wants is to be a kitchen cat and sit by the fire and mind the baby and keep the mice down. So he sets out to find a good home, but has bad luck almost everywhere. The farmer's wife thinks he's eaten the cream (though it was a hobgoblin), the Mayor's wife is frightened of all cats, a Sea Witch tries to wreck the ship when he's the sailor's cat, and the Princess he loves is sent away to boarding school. In fact, he has lots of disappointments and has to be 'de-witched' before he manages to find a happy home.

Here he is trying to be Dog Toby in a Punch and Judy Show:

●

Gobbolino left the town as quickly as possible and trotted down the country lanes.

Often he stopped a passer-by to ask politely:

'Please, sir, or ma'am, can you tell me, has a Punch

and Judy show passed this way?' and often he had the answer:

'Why, yes, my little cat. I saw it playing on the village green back yonder. You will certainly catch it up if you trot fast enough.'

And Gobbolino trotted as fast as his paws would carry him to the next village and the next and the next.

At the entrance of every village he was sure to ask:

'Please, has a Punch and Judy show been here lately?'

And he always had the answer:

'Why, yes, my little cat, it was here only yesterday. You will certainly catch it up if you trot fast enough.'

At last in the distance he saw a crowd gathered under a tree, and there sure enough was the striped showbox, and the gaudy figures of Punch and Judy.

But they were not playing today to an eager crowd. The show-people sat around sad and despondent. Some bent their heads on their hands, while others stared into the distance, saying nothing at all. It was a pitiful sight to behold, and Gobbolino lost no time in asking a woman on the outskirts of the crowd what the matter could be, and whether he could give them any help in their distress.

'Our dog Toby has died!' the woman told him, wiping away a tear. 'And of course Punch and Judy cannot perform without him. We shall all be ruined.'

'Oh dear! Oh dear! That is very sad!' said Gobbolino

with much sympathy. 'I was just about to join your show and travel the country with you, but I see now I shall hardly be wanted since there is not a show any longer.'

The woman looked him up and down. Then she called the showman, who was gloomily mending a rent in the show-box.

'Dandy! Dandy? Come here and look at this kitten! He talks of joining our show. Why shouldn't he take Toby's place and go along with us? With a ruff round his neck, who is to notice? Only a black face instead of a white, and such beautiful blue eyes! He may save our fortunes yet!'

Dandy the showman stared at Gobbolino and finally said:

'Well, why not? He looks pretty enough and clever enough, and if we have no Toby we shall be ruined. Will you do your best for us, little cat with the blue eyes, if we give you a home in our company?'

'That I will gladly, master!' said Gobbolino in delight, so the showman's wife dressed him up in a paper ruff and a blue jacket and popped him into the striped show-box with Punch and Judy and the policeman and the baby.

At first these were very ready to be jealous of him and to dislike him, but when they saw how modest Gobbolino was, how sweet-tempered, and how eager to ask: 'Should Dog Toby act like this? or like this?' they soon became friendly in return, and it was the

gayest company in the land that set forth again presently to entertain the next village they could find.

Crowds gathered the moment that the striped show-box came into sight:

'Here's the Punch and Judy! Here's the Punch and Judy!'

Dandy the showman would halt on the village green and set up the box. Soon Punch and Judy were at their tricks and the crowd were roaring with laughter, but it was always the dog Toby who was asked for again and again: 'Toby! Toby! Show us Dog Toby! Oh, what a clever fellow he is, and what beautiful blue eyes he has!'

Gobbolino acted so well, and entered into his part so eagerly that there was always a whole capful of silver at the end of the show.

The showman's children had new shoes, his wife wore bracelets, and the showman himself wore a yellow waistcoat.

'And all thanks to you, my little friend!' he would

say, affectionately, rubbing Gobbolino under the ears. 'What do you say to joining the show for good – eh? A cat might have a worse home, after all.'

'I will gladly stay with you for ever, kind master!' Gobbolino replied at once, for strange as were his new surroundings after the luxury of the palace, he found his new life as pleasant as he could wish for.

He enjoyed watching the crowds gather as the striped Punch and Judy went from village to village. He enjoyed the grins that widened on the children's faces when he and Punch popped up in the box. He loved to see the careworn faces of the old men and women, the worried faces of mothers, break into smiles as they forgot their troubles in following his tricks.

'Really there is nothing so pleasant as making people happy!' said Gobbolino. 'I shall be perfectly content to stay here for ever – Gobbolino the performing cat.'

He often wished the little princess could watch his acting. He had secret hopes that one day the showman might find his way to the boarding-school, or to the orphanage gates, or even to the nursery of the little brothers, and meanwhile he was very happy, particularly in the evenings when the show-people put up their little tents round a blazing camp-fire and Gobbolino sat peacefully beside it, his paws tucked under his chest, as content as the sleekest tabby on a kitchen hearth.

'At last I have found my home!' he said to himself. 'Who would ever have believed it would be such a strange one? But what matter? For here I am.'

One day they came to a village that was less pleasant than the rest.

The houses were grey and dirty. No flowers grew in the gardens, which were full of weeds. The street was littered with rubbish, while the pond on the village green was thick with duckweed and slime.

Nobody came out to greet the Punch and Judy show when the showman put up his striped box on the green.

A few children, slouching home from school, stared rudely but went home to tell their parents, for just as the showman was about to move on, a few people began to straggle up and stood about in little groups to watch the show.

The showman would willingly have left such disagreeable people behind, but being a merry-hearted man himself, he thought he had better do all he could to cheer their misery, so he set Gobbolino beating a drum and drew up the curtain.

The children and their parents watching did not clap their hands as most children did.

Instead, they began to make rude remarks.

'Punch has cracked his nose! Judy's pinny is torn! Look at Toby's face! Whoever saw a black Dog Toby before?'

'The old show-box could do with a clean! And the

showman too, I daresay!'

'And Dog Toby, he's black enough!' shouted someone else.

All the children laughed, but it was very disagreeable laughter.

Suddenly a voice from the back called out:

'That isn't a dog at all! It's a cat!'

Gobbolino bristled all over with rage, and the voice called out again:

'It's a cat, I tell you! And what is more it is a witch's cat, or I am very much mistaken.'

The crowd turned round to stare at the ugly old

crone who stood at the back, leaning on her stick and croaking out her words with an ugly leer.

'Old Granny Dobbin ought to know! She's a witch herself!' cried the children in chorus.

The showman began to pull down the little curtain to close the show, but the children would not be quieted.

'A witch's cat! A witch's cat!' they sang. 'Take off his ruff and let us see the witch's cat!'

They made a path for old Granny Dobbin and pushed her to the front.

'Speak to the witch's cat, Granny!' they shouted. 'Make him speak to you! Make some magic for us!'

'Ha! Ha!' croaked the old woman, pointing her finger at Gobbolino. 'I know you! Grimalkin was your mother! Your little sister Sootica is apprenticed to a witch, way up in the Hurricane Mountains! *You* a Dog Toby, indeed! Ho! ho! ho!'

The fathers and mothers of the children, standing behind, grew threatening, and shook their fists at the showman.

'How dare you bring a witch's kitten into our village?' they cried. 'How dare you harm our children so? They might be turned into mice, or green caterpillars, or toads! If it hadn't been for old Granny Dobbin here, goodness knows what might have happened! Away with you directly!'

'Out of the village! Chase them out of the village!' clamoured the children, picking up sticks and stones, and they all became so angry and pressing that the showman lost no time in packing up his box and preparing to depart.

Gobbolino, his ruff taken off, did all he could to explain himself to the angry villagers, but nobody would listen to him except old Granny Dobbin.

'It's no good, my poor simpleton!' she said when he had finished his story. 'Nobody will ever keep you for long. Once a witch's cat always a witch's cat. You will never find the home of your dreams while your eyes are blue and sparks come out of your whiskers.'

'I have met plenty of kind people in the world!' said Gobbolino stoutly. 'I feel sure that one day I shall find the home I am looking for.'

●

Don't worry, Gobbolino *does* find a home! You can meet him again in *The Further Adventures of Gobbolino and the Little Wooden Horse*.

ACKNOWLEDGEMENTS

The Editor and Publishers gratefully acknowledge the following, for permission to reproduce copyright material in this anthology, in the form of extracts and illustrations taken from the following books:

The Last Slice of Rainbow by Joan Aiken text copyright © Joan Aiken Enterprises Ltd, 1985, illustrations copyright © Margaret Walty, 1985 (Jonathan Cape Ltd); *The Little Girl and the Tiny Doll* text copyright © Aingelda Ardizzone, 1966, illustration copyright © Edward Ardizzone, 1966 (Puffin Books, 1979); *The Railway Cat and the Horse* text copyright © Phyllis Arkle, 1987, illustrations by Lynne Byrnes copyright © Hodder and Stoughton Ltd, 1987 (Hodder and Stoughton Ltd); *Olga Takes Charge* text copyright © Michael Bond, 1982, illustrations copyright © Hans Helweg, 1982 (Kestrel Books Ltd); *Milly-Molly-Mandy Stories* copyright © Joyce Lankester Brisley, 1928 (George G. Harrap and Co. Ltd); *Mr Majeika* text copyright © Humphrey Carpenter, 1984, illustrations copyright © Frank Rodgers, 1984 (Kestrel Books, 1984); *Ramona and Her Mother* text copyright © Beverly Cleary, 1979, illustrations copyright © Alan Tiegreen, 1979 (Hamish Hamilton Children's Books); *Fantastic Mr Fox* text copyright © Roald Dahl, 1970 (Unwin Hyman Ltd), illustrations copyright © Jill Bennett, 1973 (Penguin Books Ltd); *Tottie: The Story of a Dolls' House* (first published by Michael Joseph as *The Dolls' House*) copyright © Rumer Godden, 1947, 1963, 1983 (Macmillan, London and Basingstoke); *Tales from the Wind in the Willows* by Kenneth Grahame, illustrations copyright © Margaret Gordon, 1985 (Puffin Books, 1985); *The Shrinking of Treehorn* text copyright © Florence Parry Heide, 1971, illustration copyright © Edward Gorey, 1971 (Holiday House Inc., 1971 and Puffin Books, 1975); *Finn Family Moomintroll* copyright © Tove Jansson, 1948, English translation copyright © Ernest Benn Ltd, 1950 (A. & C. Black Ltd and Farrah, Straus & Giroux, Inc.); *Albert* text copyright © Alison

Jezard 1968, illustrations copyright © Margaret Gordon, 1968 (Victor Gollancz Ltd); *George Speaks* text copyright © Dick King-Smith, 1988, reprinted by permission of A. P. Watt Ltd, illustrations copyright © Judy Brown, 1988, reprinted by permission of Penguin Books Ltd (Viking Kestrel); *No More School* text copyright © William Mayne, 1965, illustration copyright © Peter Warner, 1965 (Hamish Hamilton Children's Books); *The Worst Witch* copyright © Jill Murphy, 1974 (Allison & Busby); *The Battle of Bubble and Squeak* text copyright © Philippa Pearce, 1978, illustrations copyright © Alan Baker, 1978 (André Deutsch Ltd); *Mrs Pepperpot in the Magic Wood* text copyright © Alf Prøysen, 1968, this translation copyright © Hutchinson Junior Books Ltd, 1968, illustrations copyright © Björn Berg, 1968 (Hutchinson Junior Books Ltd); *About Teddy Robinson* copyright © Joan G. Robinson, 1954 (George G. Harrap and Co. Ltd); *Captain Pugwash and the Pigwig* copyright © John Ryan, 1991 (Viking Children's Books); *Clever Polly and the Stupid Wolf* copyright © Catherine Storr, 1955 (Faber and Faber Ltd); *Danny Fox* text copyright © David Thomson, 1966, illustrations copyright © Guvnor Edwards, 1966 (Puffin Books); *The Owl Who Was Afraid of the Dark* by Jill Tomlinson text copyright © the Estate of Jill Tomlinson, 1968, illustrations by Joanne Cole copyright © Methuen & Co. Ltd, 1968 (Methuen & Co. Ltd); *Gobbolino the Witch's Cat* copyright © Ursula Moray Williams, 1942 (George G. Harrap and Co. Ltd).